Tatter and Shine

by

JW Troemner

First Edition April 2017.

Copyright © 2017 by JW Troemner.

Cover by Victoria Cooper.

For Andrew

who built me a castle

Chapter One

*O*nce upon a time, or so the story goes, a man found a demon dying on the crossroads, a holy knight's sword pinning it to the earth. It begged the man for help, as it had all who came before. And in exchange, it would give him a golden ring.

"Save me," it said, "and you will have power beyond your imagination. Save me, and you will have riches untold. Save me, and you will never die."

He feels the summoning like a pull at his navel, coaxing and cajoling him. For now it's still sweet, but it grows more insistent with every minute that it goes ignored. If he resists long enough, it will become a constant pain, knotting his stomach and yanking at his consciousness until the summoner gives up on the spell entirely. That could take hours.

Better to give in and get it over with.

He isn't unaccustomed to the feeling. Thanks to the Sorcerer Queen and her campaign to conquer half the continent, the entire region is in a constant state of upheaval. Barely a week goes by without him being summoned by one kingdom or another to solve their petty disputes. It isn't always a complete waste of his time, of course. Sometimes he picks up a few trinkets along the way, usually trophies won by strong-jawed champions while they're off being heroic across the countryside.

Who knows, this might be an entertaining diversion. If nothing else, he could take the opportunity to stock up on hen's teeth. And so he submits to the summoning and allows himself to be pulled in by its call.

When he opens his eyes, he's in the standard summoning circle, drawn in sand and chalk on a wooden floor. The floor and circle are both of passable quality, but neither is anything particularly impressive. Whatever kingdom this is, it clearly can't afford to retain a decent carpenter any more than it can an experienced sorcerer. No chance of finding anything useful here.

At least he's answered the call, which means he can leave without the summon trying to pull him back. He's about to turn around and return home again when he looks past the circle, and he realizes his error.

This isn't a palace or a castle, it's a *bedroom*. Not even a royal bedroom; at best, it might belong to a middling liege lord—a baron, perhaps? It's difficult to tell exact status, though judging by the size and furnishings, it isn't even the master bedroom. There aren't any sorcerers here, just a young woman in an expensive gown, her black hair pulled back into an elaborate coiffure, her sleeves hitched up to her elbows, with sand and chalk clinging to her hands and a look of determination in her dark eyes.

Most people cringe or shriek the first time they look at him, and not for nothing: he looks monstrous enough, with hair like lake weeds and skin like a drowned man and a shadow that pools around his feet like a puddle of spilt ink. Sometimes master sorcerers will use him as a warning to their apprentices when they think he can't hear: *look, child, and see why you mustn't delve too deep into magic. See what it will make of you.*

As if the likes of *them* could ever achieve his power.

The young woman clears her throat. It seems she isn't keen on being ignored.

"O Magister," she says, chanting the words like a recitation. "By might and magic I have summoned you here, and you will serve me—"

He laughs—a high, sharp sound like broken glass scraping across itself. "No, you haven't."

She stops short, her train of thought lost. At least she regains herself fairly quickly. "I have. I've summoned you here—"

"You might have given the order, but that doesn't mean you're the one who summoned me. Where are your sorcerers? Did you send them off to give us a bit of privacy?"

Her cheeks darken with outrage. "There are no other sorcerers in this country. I'm the one who summoned you, and I invoke the powers of Ahlasadara to—"

"You did?" He has no interest in her invocation; such things have no power over him, beyond that obnoxious pull on his gut. Curiosity, on the other hand, holds him in a tight grip. "On your own?"

"You say it like I'm a child."

"Why not? You can't be more than... twenty?" he guesses. It's always hard to tell with nobility. For peasants and craftsmen, their age is etched into their skin by years of sun and hard labor. This girl's face is pale and smooth from years spent indoors;

her uncalloused hands could belong to a girl half her age, and they'll be no different when she's fifty.

"My age doesn't matter," she snaps. "I have studied the books of Corian and Aloksamar, I have practiced the Arts, I have summoned you here, I hold you in my power, and I am *tired of being interrupted.*"

His chuckle stretches for longer than necessary, but he makes a show of keeping his lips sealed. He's glad he came after all. This is so much more fun than rooms full of droning acolytes tripping over their own clumsy spells.

"Very well," he says, long after she's finished speaking. "You've summoned me all this way. What is it you want of me, then? Do you have a curse that needs lifting?" That happens unfortunately often these days—envoys to the Sorcerer Queen rarely return to their homelands intact. "A monster problem, perhaps. Or maybe you'd like to inflict a monster problem on a rival?"

"I didn't summon you here to be my assassin," she says, still holding his gaze. She hasn't looked away once since he arrived. "You're here to be my teacher."

"Oh?" He steeples his fingers together. "You've made quite a mistake, then. The grimoires are full of demons ready to impart their wisdom, but I'm not one of them. Might I recommend Crokel? He'd be more than happy to teach you a bit of geometry, if you asked nicely. Stolas might tell you a thing or two about astronomy. Or Bifrous—"

"I've read the grimoire," she says, and he notes the singular noun. Poor dear, did she think there was only one? "If I needed the likes of them to be my teacher, then I would have summoned them, but I didn't. I want *you* to teach me magic."

"Do you now?" he asks, striding forward. "And what makes you think the likes of *you* can command *me*?"

He already knows the answer, of course. Those silly books she's read might give her power over a lesser demon like Oze or Valefar, but he's nothing like them. *They're* bound by infernal law. *They* were never human.

He reaches the edge of the chalk circle. A binding spell is built into the summoning and it hangs in the air around him like a spider's web, invisible and just as fragile. It breaks apart the second he steps through it, clinging to his skin in a feeble attempt to keep him contained.

For the first time since he arrived here, the young woman looks afraid, but only for a moment. Her eyes narrow and her jaw clenches.

"Fine," she says. "Then how about we strike a bargain instead?"

"A bargain?" He bears down on her, watching as the pallor of fear fights against an indignant flush. "Dear girl, what could you possibly have that I want?"

"A needle," she says.

"And what would I want with a magic needle?"

She glares. "It isn't magic. And even if it was, you wouldn't know what to do with it." She rights herself. "If you teach me magic, then I'll teach you to sew and weave and spin. It's clear that you can't—otherwise you wouldn't be such a tatterdemalion.

That's how it works, isn't it? You can't magic up something you can't already do."

That catches his attention, more than her projected courage or her absurd vocabulary. It's a rule of magic not often stated aloud, and even more rarely is it recorded in books. There are would-be sorcerers who go their entire lives struggling against spells they'll never be able to cast because they don't grasp that fundamental law.

Either the girl tracked down someone who was willing to tell her, or she inferred it on her own. Either way, she's resourceful.

He could use an apprentice to lighten his workload. He wouldn't say no to a few more skills, either, or clothes that aren't on the verge of falling apart.

"And what if I enjoy being a tatterdemalion?" he sniffs daintily.

"Then at least you'll be warm while doing it."

"Fair enough," he says, and lets the coyness slide. "Gather your things, then. We leave immediately."

She seizes a bag that's sitting on her dresser. "I already have everything I need."

"Everything?" He allows the word to stretch out invitingly between them.

As though she's just remembered something, she darts back to her desk and pulls out a piece of crisp paper, covering it with a clean, fine script and the scent of her anxiety. He only glances the first lines.

My dearest Father,

Try to understand—

A frivolous thing. He turns his back on her, unlatching the window. He was summoned into a room on the third story of a manor house, by the look of things. Immediately underneath the window is a fountain, shallow enough that she likely wouldn't survive if she fell from this distance. Roses are in full bloom around its base, their brilliant petals floating in the water. He wonders if they might keep the servants from noticing a body right away.

Judging by the way she's looking at him now, he isn't the only one who's entertained that thought. Perhaps she's thinking of pushing him out of her window right now.

"That's everything," she says, folding the paper with a single sharp motion and setting it on her bedside table. "What do I do now?"

He flashes a wide grin and extends his hand. "Now you come with me."

She accepts it, joining him beside the windowsill. She narrows her eyes, searching for who even knows what. A chariot of fire, some of his apprentices have told him. A golden carriage drawn by miniature dragons. Maybe a winged horse.

But the thing he chooses to ride isn't something they can see.

Before the ink is dry on her letter, he leaps from the window, still clutching her hand. For half an instant she resists—they always do—but then she leaps after him.

He grabs her tight as they hurtle through the air, the shallow fountain rushing up to meet them. But before they can hit the ground, they're caught by a burst of wind. It pulls at her skirt and at his hair, roaring in their ears as it whisks them higher than the tallest trees. Farmland becomes a patchwork quilt underneath them, stitched together by threads of brown and cobblestone gray.

The young woman doesn't scream, but it looks like she might like to. Her grip is so tight around his hand that if he were human, he might worry about bruising and lost circulation, but he doesn't release her, and the wind doesn't let them fall until it delivers them to the highest window of the tallest tower of his castle.

He dismounts elegantly, stepping onto the windowsill and hopping to the floor beneath with practiced ease. She falls in a heap beside him, shaking and wheezing.

Her long dark hair hangs loose, pulled halfway out of its elaborate coif, and her clothes are tousled beyond any sense of modesty.

"That—that was—"

"Only the wind," he says cheerfully. "Feed it and bridle it and it will take you to all corners of the earth, and quickly, but it will never be gentle."

"Oh. I…" She's still gasping. "I see."

He tsks at her. "Dear, if you're going to faint, I suggest you wait until I show you your room. If I've got to carry you around like a basket of posies, I might as well turn you into one first."

She forces herself upright. "I'm not going to faint," she snaps, proud despite her heaving chest. "And my name isn't dear, it's—"

"I don't recommend it," he says. "Names are power. Don't give yours away lightly, not even to me."

"It's a bit late for that, don't you think? Half a dukedom knows mine."

"Then you had better hope they forget it, or you. Or spend your days in a place where none can connect who-you-were to who-you-are."

"That's entirely unreasonable. You're asking me to never see my family again."

"Why?" he asks. "Did you intend to? That letter of yours certainly implied otherwise." He shrugs and steps past her. "I'm asking nothing of you. I'm simply telling you how to survive. Ignore me, if you're so inclined, but don't say I didn't warn you. But if you'd rather your lessons end here—"

She squeezes her eyes shut for a moment. When she opens them again, she is resolute.

"I have every intention of staying." She lets out a hard breath and composes herself as much as she can with her hair flying away in all directions and the hem of her skirt still hitched up to her thigh. "And what about you? What am I supposed to call you? Magister?"

He wrinkles his nose in disgust. "Like a petty court magician? Hardly."

"Would you prefer simply 'you'?" she asks flatly.

"Don't be absurd," he waves her off. "If you must address me, you can call me..." Oh, what was that word she used? Pretentious enough that she hoped he wouldn't know to be insulted. "Tatterdemalion."

The young woman's composure falls. "You…
you're not serious."

"My dear, I would never lower myself enough
to be serious about anything. Sincere, though:
absolutely."

"Tatterdemalion," she repeats, with all the
mortification of a princess who knows she's done
this to herself. "I'll make sure to remember that."

As though she could ever forget.

"And what about me?" she asks. "Do I get to
choose a name for myself, too?"

He just grins at her, showing off all his teeth.
"Shall we begin your tour?"

It's short, as tours go. The castle is a small one,
barely more than a pile of stones meant to protect a
valley that had strategic importance a few hundred
years ago. It passed into Tatterdemalion's hands by
means of a vain marquis with a need for many
favors and a shallow understanding of fine print.
Since that time, he's taken up residence in the old
marquis' spacious personal chambers, just below
what has become an alchemical laboratory. Beyond
that: a courtyard, a dining hall, a library. There are

other rooms, but he has no patience for their intended purposes. He has no guests to entertain, no faith for a chapel, no guards to house. The rooms once meant for such mundanity are instead filled with the collected treasure of a thousand and one deals, and the equipment to help him procure more at a moment's notice.

His new apprentice will be staying in the servant's quarters, situated high in a tower and connected to the kitchen, pantry and wine cellar by a narrow stair.

It's the same room where all his apprentices sleep, when he has them. They come to him time and time again: other sorcerers' apprentices who lose patience with their masters' teaching, young peasants who dream of more than a life behind a plow; children of nobles with ambitions beyond their parents' means. Some are meek and obedient; some are bright-eyed and optimistic; some silent and sad; some, like this girl, are haughty and indignant. All of them are driven, all of them determined, and eventually, all of them leave.

He watches with some interest as this one unpacks her belongings; it's always educational to see what they choose to bring. In her case, it's practical and plain, to the degree that a young woman of noble birth can be: a few simple dresses, her brushes and hairpins, some lotions and oils. She has the sense not to bother with trinkets and jewelry, though he does notice gold coins stitched into the hems of her clothes, just in case.

Clever girl.

Chapter Two

She's seen all sorts of riches in her home, but none like these. Crowns and jeweled necklaces are shelved beside quill pens and oil lamps, and with the same obvious disregard. More treasures are suspended from the ceiling, hanging from hooks at the end of long chains. One in particular catches her eye: it looks like some kind of animal hide, easily large enough to belong to a steer, but covered in large, thick scales. Perhaps it's the layer of dust that's accumulated on them, but the scales' original color seems to shift between sandy brown and dusky black. Frowning, she reaches out to brush the dust away for a better look.

"I suggest you refrain," Tatterdemalion tuts, leaning uncomfortably close over her shoulder. "That's hydra skin, you know. Poisonous as a vain hope. Touch the wrong side and you'll be dead in hours."

She draws her hand as if the hide tried to bite her. "If it's so toxic, then why do you keep it around?"

"It's hardly going to harm me, now is it? An unsuspecting thief, though..." He chuckles, long and dark. "In these rooms, you'll touch nothing unless I've said so, and only as I've said."

She glances around at the rest of the collection, scrutinizing it with narrowed eyes, but if there's any difference between the mundane and the magical, she can't tell with a look. When she glances back, the table at Tatterdemalion's side is covered with supplies: stained leather work gloves, a soft-bristled brush, cleaning cloths, and a jar of balm.

But that can't be. She's certain they weren't there a moment before, and he didn't move an inch while her back was turned. She wants to ask how he did it, but stops herself before the words are formed. She already knows the answer he'll give.

"What's all of this?" she asks instead.

"My first task for you," he says. "You're going to clean the hydra skin."

She looks back at the hide, staring it down like it might come to life and lunge at her. Knowing this place, it just might. "You said it was poisonous."

"Oh, tremendously so," he snickers. "Which is why you're going to do precisely as I say. Put the gloves on. Go ahead."

She reaches out, her hands hovering over the gloves without quite daring to touch them. Have these been used to clean the hydra skin before? They're certainly filthy enough. Did any of the toxin leach into them?

"Either do as I say or leave. Don't waste my time."

Grimacing, she picks up the gloves, pulling them tight over her hands. "Alright, what next?"

He talks her through each step of the chore, guiding her in the proper way to lay out the hide across the table, to sweep the brush with the flow of the scales, to condition the leather to keep it supple and strong. He continues talking between the instructions:

"Hydra skin is valuable in treasure chests, moppet, to kill the thieves who don't know the safe places to touch."

"It must be reconditioned every three months, or else the hide will dry and the scales will fall away—and if that happens, there'll be nothing between you and the poison."

"It's the blood that's toxic. If you want to kill a hydra, you must learn to do it from a distance."

By the time she returns the hide to its hook, the scales have an iridescent shine, like polished pearls under deep water. Tatterdemalion gives her a few seconds to admire her handiwork. Only a few, though.

"Very good," he says, and for half a moment she beams with pride. "Now for the table."

She blinks at him. "What about it?"

"What do you mean, what about it?" he asks. "It's been soaking in toxins all this time, hasn't it? Scrub it clean." He gestures impatiently at a bucket full of sudsy water and a scrubbing brush, neither of which were there a few moments before.

Her face falls. It's one thing to prepare something as arcane as hydra leather, but this is servant's work. She's never scrubbed a table in her life.

"Too much for you, is it?"

She huffs indignantly and seizes the brush, scouring the wood with determined ferocity. When she looks up and sees a block of beeswax waiting for her, she doesn't even bother to protest. She merely picks it up and begins working the wax into the table, exactly according to instructions. By the time she's finished, the surface is glossy and gleaming.

It's only good breeding that restrains an aggravated sigh when she looks down again to see a mop, a broom, and a fresh bucket of suds waiting at her feet like a trio of spaniels.

"Let me guess," she says. "I'm to clean the floors in this room, too?"

"Don't be silly." Tatterdemalion sits on the freshly polished table. "There are far too many delicate things for you to break here. No, you'll be sweeping and mopping the floors in the rest of the castle. *Excluding* the laboratory and treasure rooms."

Her mouth hangs agape for precisely half a second before it snaps shut like she's trying to bite her words in half. "That's three whole floors!"

"Yes, it is."

"It'll take me hours!"

He grins with all his teeth. "Then I suggest you hurry."

She lets out an infuriated shriek, but before he can point her to the door, she grabs the broom and marches off. Tatterdemalion's laughter follows her until he's entirely out of sight.

It does indeed take hours to sweep and mop all the castle's floors. By the time it's finished, her hands are blistered and red, the moon is rising, and she's hissing words more becoming of a sailor than the daughter of a duke. In her mind's eye, she can almost see the looks on her sisters' faces if they were here with her now. Temperance would be quietly disappointed in her language. Piety would be wailing about opportunities lost—suitable men are in short enough supply already. How could she ever make a decent match with the hands of a scullery maid?

Fortunately, they aren't here to see her. She has no family here to please, no servants to keep in line, no suitors or allies to impress. She's alone in this castle with nothing but a mop, a bucket, and the world's most powerful and irritating sorcerer, and if he thinks he can chase her off by making her mop floors, then by all that is holy, she will mop floors until her hands are bare bone.

"Well?" she asks when she's finished, thrusting the mop at him like a challenge. "Have you got anything else for me?"

Tatterdemalion meets her challenge with glee. He sets her on the laundry, and then the dishes, and then on polishing his mountains and mountains of silver. With each task he looms over her shoulder, barking instructions until she does it right.

Her body gives out before her will.

She wakes up just as the first fingers of sunlight reach through the castle windows. She never made it into bed, and now she's slumped over the table in the servant's quarters, her arms wrapped protectively around a silver pitcher. Her hair is a tangled mess sticking into the edges of her vision, and she can feel it clinging to a dried line of spittle that seeps from the corner of her mouth. Her sleeves are stained with mop water and silver polish.

She tries to pick up the pitcher and push it away, but it hurts to move. Her knuckles are scraped bloody, her hands are swollen with blisters, and her fingers are stiff. Her whole body is sore and aching.

And worst of all, she isn't alone.

Tatterdemalion sits on the other side of the table, wearing a pauper's clothes and a mocking grin and looking unnervingly like he crawled out of the bottom of a pond to drown her.

"Good morning, Shine," he trills, giving the last word an odd weight.

She narrows her eyes. "Is that what you're calling me?"

"Fetching, isn't it? It came to me last night while you were polishing the silver—which you still haven't finished, I notice."

"Of course not. It'll take days to polish all of this."

He waves her off. "No matter, you can do the rest tonight. But first, you have chores to do."

She wants to slap that smile off his face. Instead she peels herself off the table and sits upright as quickly as her aching muscles will allow. "Do I have to start right away?"

"If you came here to loaf, you're going to be sorely disappointed."

"I'm not loafing, I'm starving. You didn't let me have supper last night."

"I didn't *let* you?" he scoffs. "Did I ever stop you? No. You insisted on continuing on an empty stomach. Far be it from me to interrupt your work if you're not hungry."

She grits her teeth. "Well, I'm hungry now."

"I'm sure you are. What do you want me to do about it?"

She inhales, the demand ready and waiting on her tongue, but she leaves it there. When she does speak, she chooses her words carefully. She came here to learn magic, after all. "Is there a spell for preparing food?"

"Of course there is," he says. He doesn't elaborate.

"Will you teach it to me?"

"Oh, you know better than that." His voice lowers from that grating laugh, and he leans close over the table. "I could teach it to you, but it wouldn't do you an ounce of good. You have to know how to make it yourself. You have to know the feel of the knife in your hands, the heat of the fire, the smell of the roasting meat and the rising bread. You must be so practiced at the task that you could do it with your eyes closed. And then—only then—will you be able to perform the task with magic. If shortcuts are what you're after, then you're better off hiring servants to do it for you. Or taking an apprentice." He snickers again, and suddenly she remembers to be irate.

"So what do I do, then?" she demands.

He grins. "Get down to the kitchen and get acquainted. Make enough for two. After our breakfast, we'll see to your end of the bargain."

Shine finds fresh bread in the pantry, along with a barrel of apples and a wedge of cheese wrapped in wax cloth. It's an insultingly simple meal, but it's all she can muster the energy to prepare, and she can stack it all on a tray and carry it to the dining hall in one go.

Every part of her hurts; she can hardly keep her grip on the knife, and it shakes in her hand as she tries to cut the apple. In the end, hunger wins out over pretense, and she bites into it with a satisfying crunch. Her sister Glory would say it's behavior unbecoming a woman of her station, but Tatterdemalion doesn't seem to notice, let alone care. He spends most of their breakfast needling her for a list of supplies he'll need to procure. When they finish, he vanishes, leaving her to clean up the dishes.

The remains of the meal aren't the only mess she has to deal with. She hasn't had a chance to wash since she arrived in this castle, and a day of being thrown about by the wind and doing menial chores has left her filthy. She'll need a bath later to wash away the sweat and grime, but the mere thought of hauling that much water up so many steps is enough to exhaust her. Still, she refuses to go the rest of the day without at least washing her face and hands.

She marches to the well, grits her teeth, and hauls up the bucket a few inches at a time. It's absolutely miserable, but every twinge hardens her resolve to steel. She thinks on what Tatterdemalion said and sets herself back on the task. All the while she focuses on the chill that hangs in the well, the ache in her muscles as she pulls it out, the smell of moisture and wet stone. When the bucket emerges, she thinks about the weight of it in her hands, the way it resists as she drags it past the edge of the well, the sound it makes on the well cover when she sets it down. She ruminates the cool, earthy taste of it, the soothing feeling of cold water on her hands, the surge of wakefulness when she splashes it on her face.

The books she read always instructed her to think deeply on what she wanted the magic to do, to visualize the process and the results and make it a reality. None of them ever explained it like Tatterdemalion did. This feels more real. More right.

She commits that feeling to memory, too.

She takes one last moment to tug the pins and ribbons from her hair and comb it out with her fingers, tying it back into a simple braid to keep it out of her way.

All said, it only takes her a quarter hour to make herself somewhat presentable, but by the time she returns to the great hall, Tatterdemalion has returned. At his right stands a loom, a spinning wheel, a set of combs, and so much clean wool that the long banquet table could pass for a snowdrift.

He grins at her. "Shall we begin?"

"I would love to. But how am I supposed to card wool like this?" She thrusts her hands at him, showing off her blisters. They're even uglier today than they were last night. The coarse rope ripped open several of the sores, and others look ready to burst. "I'll get blood all over the wool, and then it'll be ruined."

She expects her tutor to be annoyed, but he grins, all teeth and pride, like she's answered a riddle. "We can't have that, now can we?" He reaches behind his back and procures a little jar. "Give me your hand."

She lets him take it, but she eyes the jar suspiciously, unsure of whether he pulled it out of thin air or whether he tucked it in his back pocket because he anticipated her request. Both seem equally plausible.

He gathers a glob of the salve onto his fingers and slathers it across her palm. Instantly relief washes over her, so abrupt it leaves her weak at the knees. As he kneads it into her hands, the blisters shrink into themselves and the redness fades. Even the scrapes on her knuckles feel less like open wounds and more like light scratches, barely worth notice.

"What is that?" she breathes.

"Beeswax and marigold," he hums, taking her other hand as well. "Blended with the chill of winter and the first breaths of a spring morning. It's good for skin. Good for healing."

She tries to form the words, but trips over them in silence. That's impossible, surely—no one can take cold and air and grind them into salve. But then, he *is* a sorcerer. The most powerful in the world, if the rumors are to be believed, maybe even more powerful than the Sorcerer Queen.

The thoughts drift away from her, and she doesn't pursue them. Possibility and reality don't seem to matter much in this moment. She could sit here and let him massage her hands forever.

He's moving up her hands to her wrists, rubbing the soreness out of her aching forearms when she remembers herself. She jerks abruptly, yanking her arm out of his grip.

"No further risk of bleeding on the wool, I take it?" he asks with a grin. "Then let's begin."

She pulls up a chair and sits so close beside him that their knees almost touch. She shows him how to properly hold the long, sinister combs in his hands, how to catch the wool on its tines to prevent waste, how to slide the combs against each other to draw the curls into long, soft strands that puff like clouds in his hands, and how to gather it into roving that's ready to be spun. He fumbles at first, but the task is simple enough once he learns the proper movements.

It's not long before he's sufficiently confident with the combs to instruct her in further chores, and she leaves him to clean the soot from the fireplaces and fill the basins for washing. Even after she's finished all of that, though, there are still mountains of wool gathered on the table. Tatterdemalion seems content in his chore.

She fetches a basket to gather the roving, then, almost as an afterthought, she brings down the serving set she was working on the night before. While he combs the wool, she shines the silver, just for an excuse to sit down.

For a long while the great hall is silent except for the click-clatter of the combs and the faint squeak of her polishing cloth. It's a comfortable, companionable silence.

"I used to do this with my sisters," she tells him absently, lulled by the familiar sound and smell of the chore. "On winter days, we would sit together like this for hours, spinning and talking. Sharing stories. Then they were married off, one by one. It isn't really the same, doing it alone."

Tatterdemalion hums thoughtfully, inviting her to continue. His attention is still mostly on the combs.

"I had brothers, too, but they died when I was young." She examines her reflection in a serving dish, then sets it down. "Honor—he was the eldest, after Temperance—he went to war with Father. Merit left to join the clergy a little after that, but he took ill on the way to the abbey. He never recovered."

"And your sisters?" His voice is low and soft. "Tell me about them."

"Temperance doesn't need magic to enchant you," she says, matching the cadence of her words with the rhythm of the combs. "All she needs to do is speak, and half the room is enthralled. Piety is clever and shrewd. You've never met anyone who can squeeze more profit out of less. Glory is an astronomer at heart—she married a merchant sailor, you know. Father was against the match at first, but I don't think he had the heart to refuse it. They would sit for hours talking about the stars. He built her an observatory as a wedding present."

"What about you?" he asks. "Planning to win a husband with magic?"

"Only if I'm hoping to woo a prison warden. Magic is illegal in Blackstone." She pauses, working at the serving dish in silence for a moment. "It isn't as though I don't understand why. We've seen firsthand what it can do, and Father more than most. He fought at the Siege of Nedow, you know. It..." She hesitates, lowering her voice. "It changed him."

"Nedow changed a lot of people." There's a gravity in his tone that makes her pause.

"Were you there?"

"I didn't have to be there to see the effects," he says too lightly. "Your home isn't the only one that outlawed magic afterward, after all. Though that does make me wonder, how *did* you get your hands on those books of yours?"

She recognizes the abrupt change of subject for what it is. Her father does the same sometimes when conversations start to go in directions he'd rather avoid.

"Oh, just because they were illegal didn't mean they weren't around," she says, matching his tone. "We went to the market fairly often, and Glory spent enough money buying books about the stars that nobody ever questioned when I went with her. Most of the time booksellers kept their books on magic in hidden compartments if they were heading to a country where they aren't forbidden." She grins at the memory. "But those are only the proper books. The ones meant for the black market usually have their covers replaced with something banal and mundane—I had one that was disguised as *The Annotated History of Shiran Textiles, Volume Three.* Even Piety didn't want to borrow it."

"It sounds like you were doing fairly well for yourself," Tatterdemalion observes. "And yet you summoned me. What changed?"

"I told you, didn't I?" She turns over a goblet, now bright as sunlight in her hands. "I learned everything I could about magic from the books. I needed a teacher."

He pauses his work. "You were prepared to run away with me the moment I arrived. What really changed?" In the absence of the comb, the silence is unnerving. It hangs in the air like a wisp of stray wool, just long enough to be uncomfortable.

Shine seizes another goblet and starts polishing, just to give herself an excuse to look away.

"I wasn't as careful as I should have been. Booksellers started making deliveries especially for me." It's easier to speak when she doesn't need to look Tatterdemalion in the eye. "Father caught wind of it, and he was furious. He didn't know it was me—I never used my own name, I wasn't that careless—but it was enough that he knew someone in Blackstone was practicing magic. He'd already sent for an inquisitor to start a proper witch hunt. It was only a matter of time until they found me out."

"It's bold," Tatterdemalion muses. "Studying magic right under his nose. What's the law out there? Torture to confession, and then... beheading, was it?"

"Father wouldn't hurt me," Shine says. "Not if he could get away with it. I'm sure he would try to cover it up and send me off to a nunnery where I couldn't embarrass him. It's far better than most people get." She's sure he would think it merciful: spending the rest of her life locked up and forced into silence, her every hour strictly regimented and chaperoned to make sure she repents the things she'll never regret.

She lingers in the thought for a moment too long; even now the idea of it chills her to the bone.

"Nonsense," Tatterdemalion says, breaking her from her ruminations. "How would you teach me to spin from inside a nunnery?" He flashes a smile that's warmer than it should be, but its edges are as sharp as his teeth. "If he means to send you anywhere, he'll have to deal with me."

She returns the smile, trying not to let the relief show on her face.

"Give me just a moment," she says, and she flicks a few wandering tufts of wool from her sleeves. "I need to fetch another basket."

The combs go silent as Tatterdemalion watches her leave.

Chapter Three

Filling the basins, Shine decides, is the worst chore in the world.

Mopping and sweeping isn't all that bad—less obnoxious when she's alone and can dance with the mop like it's one of her sisters' suitors at a ball. Dumping the chamber pots is disgusting, but at least the task is brief with just the two of them in the castle. For all its tedium, cooking is surprisingly enjoyable: she has ingredients and spices from half the world at her fingertips, and her tutor's eager encouragement to try them all.

But there's no redemption for hauling water. The wooden bucket is heavy enough when she has to pull it up from the well, and it only seems to grow more leaden with every stair she has to climb.

And so it becomes the first chore she infuses with magic.

She's scoured the library for spells, but Tatterdemalion assures her that the incantations themselves aren't as important as the understanding and will behind them. And will, she knows, she's got plenty.

She pulls the rope, hand over hand, thinking deeply about the strain in her tendons and the ache in the muscles, the creak and crack of the rope as it's pulled taut, the squeal of the pulley with every turn of its wheel. The whole of her mind is focused on the task, attuned to it until it is nearly a trance.

Suddenly something changes, like a loose wheel falling back into its track. In that instant, she stops feeling like she's holding the rope, but like the rope has melded with her skin. She can feel the tension straining every fiber in its length, the intimate mechanisms of the pulley and the places where the grease has worn away and metal slides against bare metal. She feels the bucket, suspended a few short feet over the water, still dripping as it swings a few feet over the water.

She tries to pull the bucket toward herself, like retracting an extended finger. It does nothing but swing sullenly, precisely where she left it.

She recognizes that feeling: *spite*.

"How dare you?" she hisses, tightening her grip on the rope. "You are going to come to me right this instant, do you understand?" She pours will and defiance into the rope and bucket, and slowly—ever so slowly— it admits defeat. It doesn't fly from the well or magically appear in her hand, but the rope moves easier over the squeaking wheel, and the bucket is lighter in her hand than it was before.

It's only a small bit of magic, but it's something. She made it bend to her will once. It's only a matter of time before she wears it down completely.

One day a stranger arrives at the door. A messenger, from the looks of him: his clothes are heavy with dust from the road, and he carries himself with the odd stride of a man accustomed to pushing past exhaustion. His horse, tied up in the courtyard, looks as weary as he is.

Shine watches him from the upper windows, trying to judge the man against her memories. She doesn't recognize him, but the cut of his cloak looks like it might be fashionable in one of the counties her father has dealings with. Has he ever visited her home? Would he be able to tell her what's happened there since she left? Would he know who she was, if he saw her?

Is it worth the risk?

She decides against it—she's stubborn, not stupid—and watches from out of sight as he ties up his horse and approaches the keep. The door swings open with an ominous creak before he can reach out to touch it, and alarm spreads down his features as he realizes it did that on its own.

Shine could hold back a laugh, but she doesn't.

By the time she sneaks downstairs, he's already meeting with Tatterdemalion. The messenger is a trembling mess while the sorcerer circles him like a hungry cat.

While they're occupied, she slips into the courtyard to tend to the horse. The castle probably had a stable once, but it's long gone. Tatterdemalion doesn't keep horses of his own, and so he doesn't bother with hay or grain to feed them, but Shine brings up a pile of apples from the larder and a clean washtub.

She sets it down in front of the horse and turns her thoughts elsewhere, letting them fall in tune with the well and all its pieces. It's easier this time; it almost feels as though the well recognizes her, but this time she doesn't address the rope or bucket. She draws a long, deep breath, and commands the water directly. It resists her at first, more adverse to defying natural law than she is to hauling it around, but she refuses to listen to its excuses. Slowly, reluctantly, the water concedes. A cool mist rises from the well, beading on the sides of the washtub before it drips down to fill it. The process is slow, and it costs far more effort than it would have simply to draw the water from the well with a rope, but it is undeniably *magic*.

"There you are, Shine."

She nearly jumps, but there's no need: Tatterdemalion is alone, and the messenger is nowhere in sight.

She recovers her composure quickly. "Are you finished?"

"Not yet. There's still work to be done before we're rid of this dolt. Care to join me?" He extends his hand with a flourish. It's a ridiculous gesture—a parody of courtly manners, more than actual sincerity—but it brings a smile to Shine's face.

The moment she takes his hand, the wind gathers them up in its grip. The first time they travelled this way, she was too stunned to make sense of what was happening. This time the journey only lasts a few seconds, but she's paying attention to the way the wind surges and whirls around them like a living thing, bucking and prancing before it deposits them on the windowsill of the highest tower.

"Watch your step." Tatterdemalion's hand is tight on hers to keep her from tipping out the window. Shine flashes a grin and hops down from the sill, landing easily on the stone floor of the tower laboratory, precisely the way he did when she first arrived.

The laboratory occupies the whole of the tower, the walls lined with round shelves that are full to bursting with bottles and jars. They rattle and shake as an excited wind fills the laboratory, but the containers are carefully secured in place, probably for precisely that reason. The stone floors are worn smooth from hundreds of years of footsteps, but the wear is uneven, and the work tables that crowd the space are propped up with thin shafts of wood to keep them from shifting.

"It seems the Earl of Thei has been striking deals with demons," Tatterdemalion says, pulling several jars off the wall. "Always a dangerous deal—never do it if it can be avoided, and it can always be avoided. It seems the bastard's gotten himself cursed."

"What kind of curse?" she asks, trailing at his heels. She knows Earl Thei—he and his sons fought alongside her father at Nedow, though only he came back alive.

"At night he turns into a beast and ravages the countryside, apparently. I'm told it's quite grisly. Bring these to the table, Shine. And fetch a clean rag to tie around your face. You don't want to breathe what we're brewing."

The chemistry is more detailed than she expected. Each ingredient has to be precisely weighed and measured, chopped up just right and added in just the right moment.

"Lotos pods for sleep," he instructs, adding a handful of what look almost like honeycombs to the crushed dryad bark in her mortar. "Grind it down to a coarse powder—that's it. Now watch your hands." He leans over her, squeezing a few drops of an acrid-smelling liquid into the stone bowl. "Dipsa blood. Incredibly toxic. Mix it well."

She does as instructed, carefully blending it into a paste. "And this will cure Earl Thei?"

"Of course not," he says. "He's cursed by demon magic. There's nothing that can save him from that but the demon that cursed him, and that will cost more than his dear heirs are willing to give."

Shine's hand goes still on the pestle. "You don't mean to kill him, do you?"

"It's hardly uncommon in this business," he says, ignoring her disquiet. "But his youngest daughter is expecting twins, and his eldest is petitioning the king for the right to inherit when her father dies. They can't risk him dying before it's all sorted."

For good reason, too. If he dies without an heir, then the Thei holdings will be divided up between anyone with half a claim, and its standing in the kingdom will be decimated. It's a process she's seen play out a dozen times in the past ten years.

"Then what is this?" she asks.

"Basilisk venom." He hands her a vial. "Add three drops, but don't let it touch anything but glass and stone. It's very important."

She dips the glass dropper into the venom and holds it over the mortar. "I mean, what is it we're making, if you can't cure him and you don't intend to kill him? What are we going to do to him?"

"Why? Having reservations?"

She sticks out her chin. "I don't need reservations to be curious."

"It won't kill him, but it will make him ill—and weak enough that the palace guards can subdue him when necessary."

"That doesn't sound terribly pleasant," she says.

"More pleasant than an axe to the head. *Three* drops, Shine."

The venom is thick and viscous, and it clings to the glass dropper with a spiteful determination. The first two drops grudgingly drip into the mortar, but the third refuses, even after she dips it back into its vial for more.

"I'm trying," she says, tapping the dry end of the stopper to encourage it. The last drop hits the mortar, but several more fall free, landing on the wooden table. Instinctively she reaches to wipe it up, but Tatterdemalion grabs her by the wrist.

"Don't touch it." He seizes the dropper from her hand and sets it back into the vial. "Get water, and quickly. As much as you can."

She hesitates, staring at the table. She could summon water right from the well. She knows she can, she just did it an hour before, but it won't answer her call. The drops of venom that had hit the table are lower than they were a few seconds before, bored into the wood as if by a drill.

"Don't just stand around," Tatterdemalion snaps. "I told you to get water!"

She gives up on the spell, running down the stairs instead. The well is too far away, so she rushes into Tatterdemalion's room, sprinting back up to the laboratory with the pitcher from his washing basin. The table is already cleared, its contents returned to the shelf and the mortar and pestle high and out of reach. The moment she gives him the pitcher, he dumps it unceremoniously onto the worktable. The whole table floods, dripping over the side.

He wrinkles his nose, stepping back just before the growing puddle can hit his boots. Agitation pours off him in waves as he hands her the empty pitcher. "Put that away and fetch the mop. I'll finish here."

"I didn't know it would do that," she said.

"Ignorance won't stop basilisk venom from eating you alive."

She nods and starts for the door, but he stops her. "Oh, and only use the mop to sop up the water. Don't touch it."

She looks up.

"It should be diluted into impotence, but that doesn't make it pleasant on bare skin."

It's weeks before Tatterdemalion lets Shine back into the laboratory. The next time, he's more thorough about explaining the ingredients and more specific in his warnings. She's far more careful than she was before, never letting so much as a drop out her sight. Still, they keep a bucket of water on hand, just in case.

In the meantime, Shine practices her magic. She learns to make the bucket of mop water follow her around the castle, and she can make the mop wring itself clean on her command. She can spark the kitchen fire with a thought, and can coax it from a roaring flame to an even smolder. Under her tutelage, Tatterdemalion learns to spin roving into thread, weave thread into cloth, and stitch the finished wool into a shirt. It's a rough garment, barely more than a shift, but with every stitch he lays the foundations for future spells.

Every morning he introduces her to another one of his trinkets, teaches her its qualities and the proper way to maintain it. Her lessons don't only extend to the contents of the treasure rooms. Each of the doors is locked with intricate spells. One requires bits of stone to be pressed in a particular order; another won't open until she plucks three hairs from her head and ties them in a loop around a wall sconce. A third requires a set of passwords that changes with the cycles of the moon. She memorizes each in turn, tucking the secrets away in the back of her head for later.

When he leaves on errands or to make his deals, she sneaks back in on her own. She's sure he wouldn't mind.

Tatterdemalion has always insisted on her being self-driven. She's the one who has to decide when to eat, when to sleep, when to incorporate magic into her chores, when to fill the pantry before it gets too low. He's never attempted to guide her in those things.

Now that she's exhausted the most interesting books from the library, she sneaks into his treasure rooms. On a shelf between a monkey's paw and a pair of dancing shoes, she finds a collection of books too valuable or dangerous to keep in the library.

And so she reads.

"The muscaliet fur in the laboratory is losing its heat," Tatterdemalion tells her over breakfast that morning. "I'll need to get fresh clippings, and a few other things besides. I won't be gone long."

But that was hours ago. The castle is as clean as Shine intends to get it, she's spent so long poring over the books in the library that her head hurts, and the last daylight is fading.

She's busy laying wood in the fireplace of the great hall when the doors burst open. A wild, turbulent squall fills the room, knocking at the tapestries on the walls and yanking at her clothes. Soot and ash billow from the fireplace, and Shine coughs, shielding her eyes in the crook of her elbow. But just as abruptly as it arrived, the gale disappears and the room is quiet once more.

She lowers her hands carefully, in case the wind decides to pick up again. But no—that was no natural wind.

That was magic.

"Tatter?" she calls out.

There's no answer.

"Tatterdemalion?" She flattens her skirt and cautiously she steps outside.

She's about to call out his name again, but it comes out as a horrified cry.

He's lying in the courtyard, slumped across the foot of the well.

She knows it's him only because of the familiar rags: the rest of him is drenched in blood. He reaches out to her with a single shaking hand.

In an instant she's got her skirts in hand and she's running to his side. She all but dives down to help him up, summoning the magic to make him light enough to carry, when he gargles out a word:

"Don't."

His shaking hand is still extended, his palm flat toward her. A signal to stay back.

It does nothing to stay the panic. "Tatter, what happened?"

"Basilisk," he says, so rough and low that it might only be a cough, but slowly the word congeals in her senses, and with it a rising horror.

She still remembers what a single drop did to an oak table.

Tatterdemalion is shuddering in agony as it does the same to him.

"Hold on." She unwinds the well rope and drops the bucket with a distant splash, commanding it to return with all the power of her mounting panic. The bucket leaps into her hands, and she pours it out over Tatterdemalion's head.

He sputters and spits as the cold water hits his face. As the blood washes away, his wounds become clear, but they don't look like anything made by claws or fangs. Part of his cheek has been eaten away entirely. Flashes of pitted, corroded bone are visible through the gaping hole in his jaw.

She stifles a cry and hauls up another bucket of water, then another. Over and over again she pours them out over him, until the last of the venom is gone and Tatterdemalion is left drenched and shivering in a pool of mud.

"Come with me," she says, willing him light enough to hold in her arms, and she carries him inside as gently as she can. The last of his rags fall away as she climbs the stairs, disintegrated by the venom and harsh water. She catches a flash of drowned-gray skin, raw meat and gleaming bone. Before she can even feel properly ill, his shadow wraps around him like a shroud, obscuring his wounds in inky black. She can still feel him, though: he's frighteningly cold as she lays him in his bed, even after she ignites the logs in the fireplace.

The window of the laboratory is wide open, and the wind tugs anxiously at her skirts as she searches through the shelves.

"It's alright," she tells it, and tries not to wonder if it's a lie. "Don't you worry about him. He's going to be fine."

She doesn't trust herself to brew unfamiliar potions—not when her pulse is racing and unshed tears are clouding her vision, not when a simple mistake could turn a healing salve into something caustic and deadly—but she still remembers the potions he's used on her. A few of them are in the laboratory, already made. She gathers as many as she can carry, and hurries back to his side.

He's curled into himself, his eyes shut, his face stony. His chest rises and falls, but each breath comes short and shallow.

Her hands tremble as she sorts through the potions, racking her mind for the ingredients in each and the instructions he gave her on how they interact. A hundred thousand warnings crowd her mind, leaving her dizzy and frantic, but they all wrap around one refrain:

He can't die like this. He can't. She won't let him.

Biting her lip, she opens the jar of marigold salve—winter's chill to soothe and spring breath for healing—and spreads it on the wounds on his face. He shudders at the cold, but he doesn't wake.

She applies more. A paste of garlic and red sap around his ribs to stave off infection. Tincture of silver and ginseng on his stomach to cure all ills. Over the fire she boils ginger root and chamomile into a tea to keep him warm. When she can't think of anything more, she wraps his wounds in gauze and covers him in blankets to stave off the chill.

She waits by his side for hours, watching for signs of change, making certain that he never stops breathing. To occupy her fidgeting fingers, she finds a needle and the shirt he's been working on, and she stitches blooms of seaweed and anemone along the collar.

The night drags on, and with each passing hour, it grows harder to keep her head upright. By the time the first streaks of pink light up the sky, she nods off entirely.

When she next opens her eyes, her teacher is gone.

She starts awake, snapped out of her doze with a surge of panic.

"Tatter?" she cries. She rushes to the bed, throwing back the blanket. It's bad enough when ordinary people get delirious with fever and pain—what could a sorcerer do? If he wanders off somewhere where she can't find him—if he gets hurt again— "Tatterdemalion!"

"I'm right here." His voice comes from right behind her. She whirls so quickly she nearly falls into him, but he steadies her easily. The grin he flashes should be more grotesque than it is, but his cheek is intact, his bone no longer exposed. He looks as healthy and hale as ever. Better, perhaps, now that he's wearing fresh clean clothes instead of the same old rags. She recognizes her embroidery around his collar, and a gold ring around his finger.

"Don't scare my like that," she snaps, and then, softer: "Are you alright? The basilisk—"

"Oh, that little thing?" He waves one hand, like being half-dissolved by venom is a mere puff of smoke. "Never you mind about that little inconvenience."

"Don't talk to me about inconvenience!" She yanks herself out of his grip, in part to hide the moisture welling in her eyes. "It almost killed you!"

His expression softens, and he reaches out to wipe a fledgling tear from her cheek. "Don't worry yourself on my account, Shine. I'm harder to kill than that."

Chapter Four

Once upon a time, a man found a demon dying on the crossroads, and the two of them made a deal. It offered him immortality, power, and a golden ring; in exchange, he gave it a home inside himself, and the man thought he had made a clever bargain.

While Shine sleeps, Tatterdemalion retreats to the solitude of his laboratory, his eyes lingering on the courtyard below. The grass is yellowed and dead where it soaked in diluted venom. He'll have to test the well later to make sure none of the poison leached into the water. In his mind's eye he can still see the look of horror on Shine's face when she found him. It's a small miracle that he managed to stop her before she touched him. If he didn't...

He pushes aside the thought, twisting the ring on his finger. None of this would have happened if he'd been wearing it when he went out. The basilisk's fangs would barely have scratched him. Its venom would have been little more than an itch on his skin.

The moment he slipped the ring out of its secret compartment and onto his finger, he began to recover in earnest. With it on his hands, he feels stronger than he has in years. He can do anything. All of reality is his to command.

To an extent.

Because the ring is several sizes larger than it was a few hours ago. It's a fickle, treacherous thing, prone to growing loose and falling from his fingers when he isn't paying attention. It already has, twice, but each time he's heard the clank of metal on stone and caught it before Shine could see. He's tried securing it by a chain around his neck, but the chain will inevitably break, or tangle in a passing branch, or slip from his neck as he rides the wind across the countryside.

And then it's only a matter of time before somebody finds it.

It happened forty-three times already, before he secured the ring behind spells and locks that even it couldn't escape. Forty-three people have held the ring in their hands and worn his life around their fingers.

Some he managed to trick into giving up the ring, offering to grant their wishes in exchange for its return. Most thought they were clever enough to refuse that offer.

One was a retired soldier with impeccable taste but no sense of scale, who thought murdering a princess' parents was the way to win her heart.

Two were an elderly couple too eager to have a child to specify where it ought to come from or what it ought to be.

One was a knight who wanted the glory for slaying monsters without any of the effort or danger.

One was a woodcutter's daughter who gave him back the ring the first time he asked for it. He liked that one—he watched over her family for three generations, arranging circumstances from the shadows to ensure that fortune was always on their side. But she was the exception. Most were too enraptured by the promise of riches and power to part with an opportunity so easily.

They never lasted long, of course. It was only ever a matter of time before they grew too confident and started giving him commands that they didn't bother to think through. The nature of the ring kept him from murdering them directly, but there was always a way. The sight of gold pouring from the windows and doors of a peasant's cottage had a habit of attracting all sorts of unpleasant people, after all.

He made the mistake of telling those stories to one of his apprentices: a young woman with an eye for things that glitter and sense of humor as sharp as a hidden knife. He called her his Magpie when he took her under his wing. He called her other things when she moved out of the tower room and into his.

When she left him, she gave herself a new name: Bryony Mhioden, first of her name, the Sorcerer Queen.

"Were you married?" Shine asks one day, watching Tatterdemalion spin thread from the first light of dawn. Now that he's got a feel for it, there's no more need to work with materials as mundane as wool, though he still wears the shirt he made for himself. It's a point of pride, more than anything else. And besides, he happens to enjoy the embroidery along the collar. "Or are you still, I suppose?"

The wheel slows. "Hm?"

"The ring," she says. "You didn't wear it before."

He shrugs her off. "It's just a trinket. Nothing of importance."

"That doesn't answer the question, though." She puts down her polishing cloth. "You know all about my family. You've never mentioned your own."

He hums again, not looking up from his work. "I don't think of them often. All dead, I imagine."

Her voice softens. "I'm sorry."

"Don't be. I'm sure at least some of them lived to ripe old age. I certainly don't lose sleep over it."

"Were they not... like you?"

He flashes a grin. "There aren't many like me, Shine. No, they were human, and they lived and died as humans do."

"Oh." She looks down, focusing on polishing the stains from a spoon while she orders her thoughts. "It's magic that made you the way you are, then?"

"In a manner of speaking."

"Is that what's going to happen to me, when I've learned enough?"

He pauses his spinning to look at her directly. "Does that frighten you, Shine? A lovely creature like yourself turned into something like me?"

She doesn't hesitate. "Of course not. I came to you to learn magic, didn't I? I'm not about to be frightened off by the consequences."

"Many are."

"Is that why you won't teach me any spells?" she asks. "Because you think I'll run off the moment I get overwhelmed?"

He snorts. "What do you mean, don't teach you? As if the mop bucket doesn't follow you around like a stray dog."

"I mostly did that on my own," she argues. "And besides, it's kitchen witchery. It isn't like combing steel ingots into roving, or bridling the wind, or—or remaking yourself after you might have died. When will you teach me to do *that*?"

His hand lingers on the spindle. He's had this conversation before, though the last time he was sitting in a different room and the beautiful woman he was talking to was sitting at his other side, setting rubies into a silver ring. His Magpie used the opportunity to ask about other jewelry, then.

He picks up the combs; if he's going to be plagued by the feeling, he might as well put it to good use later. But even while he works, one phrase bothers him.

Kitchen witchery. His Magpie called it that, too. In three hundred years of apprentices, she was the only other one.

"Shine?" he asks cautiously. "How did you know to summon me?"

"What do you mean?"

"The spell you used. It was rather particular, don't you think?" There are more than a few ways to summon him—symbols carved into trees, boxes buried at crossroads, names that he'll hear if they're said three times before a mirror—but the circle she used was more suited to calling on demons. It even came complete with a demon's binding, if an inept one.

"I wouldn't know," Shine says. "I found it in a book, I tried it, and it worked. Why? Do you intend to teach me other summonings?"

It sounds like a mere coincidence. He'd certainly taken it for one, when it happened. To a self-taught amateur, one summoning spell might have looked as effective as any other. After all, there's only one living person who knows about his connection to the ring.

"Where did you get that book, Shine?" he presses. "Who did you buy it from?"

"I've already told you, I bought my books from the market in Blackstone. Most of the booksellers never gave me their names."

A particular spell in an untraceable book in a dukedom with only one practicing sorceress. A pretty one, too. And one who would certainly need a teacher to guide her someday.

What does that sound like to you? whispers a part of him he'd rather not hear.

He doesn't want to think it, but the word forms in his mind before he can push it away: *a trap.*

Tatterdemalion waits until she's asleep, then steals away into the treasure room closest to his bedroom, the one locked with puzzles and spells to confound a thousand intrepid heroes.

The floor is piled with silks and gold. The walls are lined with the most precious and rare concoctions. Here is the sword that always severs heads, the axe that makes all things burst into flames, the spear tipped with a dragon's tooth. They're all impressive, and they catch the eye with their glamor and gleam. Nobody would ever notice the loose brick in the far corner, hidden behind a living tapestry, if they didn't already know it was there.

He pulls the brick out of its place and tucks the ring into the little compartment behind it. Kept in place by mortar and stone, the ring won't be able to slip away from him. Without it flashing in her face, Shine will forget she ever saw the damn thing.

A messenger arrives at the gate with burns on his horse's flanks and scorch marks on his clothes. While Shine tends to his horse, Tatterdemalion ushers the messenger into the library.

It doesn't take long to deduce the problem: recent warfare has driven a dragon down from the mountains, and the beast must either be driven back or destroyed before it devours half the mark. It's an unpleasant task, and not one he intends to perform cheaply. He'll need to go to the messenger's patron directly to negotiate his payment before he begins. Given how much damage the dragon has already done, it should be a quick meeting.

He sends the messenger on his way, tells Shine that he'll be leaving, and summons the wind carry him away. But before it can take him more than a few miles, a thought nags at his mind.

It *is* a dragon, after all. Creatures of such a magnitude aren't to be trifled with lightly. He's sure he could find a way to defeat it on his own, but there's no telling how long it will take, or how badly it will hurt him.

Better to fight it when he's at his full strength. Better to take the ring, just this once.

He turns back, climbing back into his castle through his bedroom window. A few quick strides take him down the hall and to the secret door that hides his treasure room.

Although it clearly isn't secret enough.

Shine is crouching over it, palpitating the wall with her fingers and muttering under her breath.

Tatterdemalion's blood runs cold. "What do you think you're doing?"

She jumps, but turns to face him with more dignity than most spies can muster. "I was looking around."

"For what?" he demands. "There's nothing in that room for you."

She digs her heels in. "I'm assuming there are books, for one," she says. "Just like in all the other rooms."

"You've searched the other rooms," he says slowly.

"Of course I have!" she says. "How do you expect me to learn anything when you keep the most important books locked away like this?"

"They're locked away for a reason."

"What difference does that make?" she demands. "For all I know this is just another one of your tests. How do I know you're not trying to make me prove myself so you'll teach me real magic—"

"Because you're never going to learn real magic," he snaps. "You keep holding out hope for a ludicrous fantasy, and it isn't ever going to happen."

"Then what am I even doing here, if you're not going to teach me?" She advances, iron in her spine. "Why am I even here, except to wash your floors and do your laundry? I'm supposed to be your apprentice, and you treat me like your scullery maid!"

"Better a scullery maid than a thief and a spy." Shine recoils like she's been slapped, but he doesn't back down, and neither does he. "Do you really think you're the first apprentice who's tried to rob me?" His voice is sharp and pitted as an old knife. "Did Bryony think that you might succeed where she failed? Tell me, Shine. Whose apprentice are you really?"

But Shine is no longer answering his questions. There's something unfamiliar in her eyes, and it's hard and cold.

"She was your apprentice," she says slowly, and he can see the realization on her face like the sun rising over a battlefield. "The Sorcerer Queen learned magic from you."

"Don't you dare—"

She strides forward, crowding out his accusations with her own. "My brother died at Nedow, and ten thousand people died with him. She has half the continent under her control, and the bandits and monsters she's summoned to do her bidding are ripping the country apart, and the rest of us are trying to subsist on the scraps, and *you*—" She looks like she might scream, but her voice pitches low instead. A quiet, deadly calm. "You could have stopped it at any time. You helped it happen."

He bares his teeth. "You know where the door is."

She draws herself up to her full height. She may have been mopping floors and cleaning out fireplaces, but she is still the daughter of a duke.

"Yes. I do."

And she turns without another word.

She arrived at his castle with a single bag of possessions. She leaves with only the clothes on her back and the shoes on her feet. When she walks away, it is with her head held high and her back straight as a lance.

She doesn't look back, not even once.

Tatterdemalion watches her leave the whole way, just to be sure.

After all these years, he didn't think he was still capable of regret.

Chapter Five

Once upon a time, a man and a demon shared a promise, but the man had heard enough of demons not to trust them absolutely.

"Eternal life seems splendid now," he said. "Less so watching my sweetheart grow old and die. Make me a promise, demon: when I send you away, you will go, and take your damnation with you."

"As you wish," said the demon. "But power draws false friends and scheming companions. Your promise is this: when you kiss the one that loves you truly, I will leave, and darken your soul no more."

Another summoning.

Tatterdemalion can feel from here that it's poorly constructed, with barely an ounce of magic behind it. The work of a complete amateur with delusions of grandeur.

Hardly worth his time, except as a diversion.

Hell only knows that he needs a diversion.

It's been a year since Shine left—or he thinks it's only been a year. He's found himself losing track of time since then. In her absence, the castle seems too big, too quiet, too empty.

When messengers come begging for his aid, all he can see is Shine's face and the accusation in her eyes. *You could have stopped it at any time.*

He takes their requests, just to get her voice out of his head. Sooner or later, he's sure he'll forget her entirely. In the meantime, he wants to hurry the process along, and if that requires answering summonings from half-wit neophytes, then so be it.

With a sigh, he submits to the call and allows himself to be transported.

Even before he opens his eyes, he's struck by the profound *wrongness* in the air. Magic is heavy and potent around him, whirling like a maelstrom before it's sucked into a bottomless void. The scent of blood hangs so thick that he can taste iron on his tongue.

The room itself is small, lit only through narrow slits in the wall, each too thin to put his arm through. The door is reinforced with iron. The stone floor is uneven, and so cold that if he were still human he would be shivering.

The circle at his feet is drawn in blood, the symbols rough and awkward, though each one has obviously been traced over several times. It took a great deal of blood to craft this. More than enough to kill its owner, if he wasn't already dead.

The body lies beside the circle. His throat is torn open, and one hand is dark with gore. His skull is dented and burned; more bruises and scorch marks cover his chest and shoulders, likely caused by the bloodstained branding iron that lays beside his corpse.

Rust-colored footprints lead away from the scene, ending in the shadows behind him.

Slowly he turns.

A young woman stands in the corner, her hair matted and her eyes sunken, dangerously skinny and sickly pale. Elaborate brands form ugly scars across her hands and feet, her knees, her face. More are visible underneath the edges of her thin, bloodstained shift.

He wouldn't recognize her at all, if not for the way she stands and the obstinate jut of her chin when she looks at him.

His blood freezes. Her name comes out a breath: "*Shine.*"

"I know we didn't part on the best of terms." Her voice is cracked and hoarse. "But I'd like to make a deal."

Tatterdemalion reaches for her, but hisses away. The mark carved deep into her skin glows with a scent of cooking meat, and Shine gasps in pain. The magic in the air grows stronger, surging around her with renewed force.

Healing sigils are set into the walls and floor. They're probably all that's keeping her alive, but just barely. As quickly as their power touches her, it's sucked into the dispelling runes that are carved into her skin, and every time those runes activate, they burn deeper.

She sways; from the look of it, stubbornness and grit are the only things keeping her on her feet. Her voice is nearly inaudible between her clenched teeth: "*Get me out of here.*"

Tatterdemalion splinters the door with a thought. Guards rush inside at the sudden sound, but they're dispatched just as quickly.

She tries to follow him, but she stumbles and falls, too dizzy with pain to see straight. The healing sigils of her cell are losing their grip on her. Soon they'll be too far away to keep her alive at all.

He gathers her up in his arms, wrapping her in his cloak to make a barrier between them. A spasm shudders through her body as he moves her. Vengeance burns in his veins, sharp and hot against the freezing horror he hasn't felt in years.

He reins in the wind and carries her back to the castle, so fast that branches are ripped from trees and thatch is stripped off rooftops as they pass. All the while Shine's pulse sputters and jumps under his fingers. Her breath comes shallow. Yellow puss seeps into his embroidered shirt as he carries her into his room and lays her across the bed.

The servant's quarters won't do. The draft alone might kill her.

He rises into his workshop, pours tinctures and elixirs and mixes up a panacea to steady her heart and stave off infection.

His hands shake. He doesn't want to know which of the miserable, useless, crippling, surging emotions is making his mind race. Maybe all of them. He can't tell anymore. When the potions are made, he cradles Shine's head in his arms and pours the panacea between her lips.

The blood in his veins threatens to burn through his skin. His eyes blaze. Raw power wraps around Tatterdemalion like a cloak. The windows shatter, the stone cracks, the wood of the bed twists and warps, and the warding runes glow white hot on Shine's skin. Still unconscious, she whimpers in pain.

He doesn't bother with the door. He strides to the window and leaps into the empty air, harnessing the wind before his stomach has a chance to catch up with him.

Tatterdemalion picks up the body with one hand. With the other he holds a vial against the fatal wound, collecting as much blood as the container will carry.

The spell only requires a few drops, but Tatterdemalion is in no mood for precision. When the vial is full, he wills a stopper into it, pockets it, and hurls the body into the pile.

The fools thought they could run.

The spell requires the blood of the one who hurt her—the ones, in this case—but he would have killed them anyway. He hunted them down, scenting them like a bloodhound when they ran, digging the truth out of them in those fleeting, screaming moments before the end. He asked over and over again, but the truth didn't change.

Patrolling soldiers found her on a country road and brought her before her father. She'd said once that she expected the mercy of a nunnery. Instead he handed her over to Bryony.

Unwilling to enter a second war with the Sorcerer Queen, he made a bargain. She could take his daughter, lock her away, bleed the magic out of her—anything she wanted, so long as she didn't kill her.

The bastard lacked imagination. Bryony never was one to tolerate a rival.

Half drunk on slaughter, Tatterdemalion steps past the pile of bodies. In his pockets jangle vials of blood—enough to fill every shelf in his tower, though they take up no room on his person, and he can't feel their weight as he walks. Only the wind protests the extra luggage as it carries him home, hissing and roaring. It gathers up the blood he didn't take and paints it across the sky, staining the dawn sun an evil red.

Tatterdemalion congratulates its artistry.

For a night and a day he combs and spins and weaves with feverish intensity. He twists blood and magic into every thread until the finished shroud glistens with raw power. It glides like silk between his hands as he carries it up the steps to his bedroom.

Shine hasn't moved—the same potion that keeps her alive ensures that she remain asleep—but she twitches as if from a nightmare. Salt tears leak from her eyes and seep down her mutilated face.

Rage wells up within him again—and with it, a note of grim satisfaction. A few more moments and the pain will end. The people who did this won't touch her ever again.

But when he unfurls the shroud over her form, it sits there, limp and useless as a bedsheet.

He leans closer, careful not to touch the scorched runes in her skin, and sees what he missed before: the spiraling letters of her true name carved into her chest, giving the wards strength and binding them to her. It's ancient magic, and it will take even older magic to undo.

Blood sacrifice and true love might do the trick, whisper the darkest parts of himself. *Her sisters could pay the toll.*

He summons a knife from the kitchen and carves it across his palm, squeezing a fist to make the blood flow. The moment it hits her skin, he can feel the wards leaching at the magic in his veins.

It has no effect.

There aren't many magics more potent than spilt blood and broken flesh. He could spend years searching the earth for an artifact that could channel that kind of power. Decades. Centuries.

He could. And he would, if it meant saving her.

Fortunately, he already has one in his treasure room.

The demon in his head fights him every step of the way, and every step it is ignored.

It snarls and spits—he doesn't listen.

It claws at the walls and tries to drag him back—he pushes past.

It stretches his shadow until the entire room is obscured by inky black—he crosses the room by memory and pushes aside the living tapestry. The loose brick comes out easily in his hand.

The demon cajoles, it reasons with him, it even begs, but it can't stop him from lifting Shine's hand and slipping the ring onto her finger, ever careful not to touch her bare skin.

Her hand warms in his—then burns with a fever heat. The air crackles and sparks as the wards on her skin splinter apart.

Hastily he replaces her hand under the shroud—he doesn't want to do things halfway, he remembers what happened with those swan boys, after all. Unhindered, the shroud seems to grow warmer, brighter, until the whole room is illuminated by its light. It melts like wax against her body, covering her with new skin—unscarred, unmarred, pink and soft in its freshness.

He watches her, his eyes never leaving her until the iron scent of pain fades into a memory. About that time he remembers that she is naked on his bed, her breasts rising and falling with every soft breath.

Perhaps waking to find him standing over her... perhaps it isn't the best way to begin a morning.

He covers her with the down comforter, smooths her hair, and remembers himself just in time.

His lips hover a hair's breadth from her forehead before he pulls away.

Tatterdemalion fights a headache while he spins. Now that the euphoria of murder has passed, the aftermath leaves his body sore and his head aching. For hours he wards it off with the soft whir of the spinning wheel. He doesn't look up until his pile of wool has dwindled to a few wisps and his spool is heavy with thread.

And then he sees her, not quite inside the chamber, her hand curled delicately around the edge of the door frame. She wears an old gown of hers—one that he believed he might have been able to trade away but could never quite bring himself to part with. Her hair is tangled and unwashed, and her eyes are wide and wary.

She's afraid of him.

"Awake at last, Shine." He keeps his voice light.

"No." She shakes her head slowly. "No, I'm not. I'm dreaming again."

As he rises to approach her, she flinches away from him, curling closer against the stone.

"I assure you, you're quite awake."

"That's what you said last time." She shuts her eyes and breathes deep, bracing herself like she expects him to lash out at her. It leaves him inexplicably angry.

"If you don't want to be here, there's the door." He points it out with a flourish, knowing full well she could navigate it in her sleep. But when her eyes open, Shine's shoulders are stiff, her jaw set, her knuckles white as she clutches the stone.

"I'm not leaving," she says. "Not this time. And you can't make me." He leans back and gives her a halfhearted scowl, but that only spurs her on. "This is my dream, Tatterdemalion. And until that sun rises—" She stabs her finger at the window— "I am not going anywhere."

Seeing her standing there— so stubborn but so afraid, staring at him like she'll strike him down— leaves him raw and hollow. Rescuing her came easy when she was unconscious, when he didn't have to look her in the eyes and see the accusation there, when he can't feel the wound in his hand like a felon's brand. The cut won't heed his magic and heal, and each throb of pain hisses through him: *This happened because of you.*

Tatterdemalion retreats into himself, wrapping himself in armor made from dramatics. "So you've been dreaming about me? Oh, do tell."

"Don't mock me," she says, and his laughter dies in his throat. He thinks it's that look in her eye or the fire in her voice. Then the glint of gold catches his eye, and he realizes his mistake.

Wrapped around her finger, secured in place by a clenched fist, is his ring.

He waves her away. "Wouldn't dream of it, Shine. Simply curious." But when he lowers his arm, her gaze follows it.

"What happened to your hand?"

He waves his arm with a flourish. "This, moppet? Nothing important."

Her face twists into concern and she marches to his side. "You can't be serious," she says. "Here, let me see it."

This time he feels the compulsion like an itch under his skin, a half-forgotten sunburn that might flare into open pain at any moment. He lays his hand in hers, and she brings it carefully to her face, studying it in the most minute detail.

"This wound looks old. Shouldn't it have closed already?"

"Magic is a tricky mistress, I'm afraid." His blood reacted poorly to the warding magic in her skin; even though the runes are gone, their effect on him hasn't entirely faded. "This is a wound it will not heal."

A twinge of discomfort crosses her features, but it vanishes with a shake of her head. "Then the old-fashioned way will have to do. I'm sure some stitches—"

He tries to pull his hand away, but the ring's magic won't let him. Instead he wrinkles his nose. "I'd rather not."

She gives him a look like he's being superbly childish, but she concedes with a roll of her eyes. "Well, at least let me wrap it. Do you have any camphor? Rosemary?" She hasn't even been out of the damned tower for a full day, barely awake for five minutes, and already she's digging her heels in. Typical. He nods, and she drops his hand like it's made of fire. "Still in your laboratory, right?"

He can only even begin to nod before she darts off like she owns the place. She's been gone for more than a year. How on earth does she remember where he keeps the camphor? How does she know he hasn't moved anything since then? For all she knows, he's added another entire wing to the castle. Magic can do that, after all.

Not that he's actually done any of that. But still. It's the principle of the thing. *He's* the master of the house.

And she's *his* master, now that she's holding the ring.

The thought sends a jolt through his stomach.

Tatterdemalion doesn't get a chance to consider further before Shine descends from the steps, entirely too many supplies piled into her arms.

"Come over here and let me take a look at it again," she says, and he's on his way to her side, pulling rolls of gauze and jars of camphor out of her arms before she can drop the whole load.

"You are allowed to rest, you know," he says flatly.

"Maybe I don't want to rest." She snatches his hand in hers and sets to work, cleaning his wound with stinging alcohol.

He lets out a sharp hiss of pain, and her gaze flicks to his face. For a moment he can see that look of fear return to her eyes.

"It hurts," he explains, his voice lower than he intended.

"It's going to sting a bit." Despite her determination, she speaks gently. "But maybe herbs and time can cure what magic won't." She watches him carefully as she spreads the camphor and rosemary over the cut. The salves send shooting pains into his hand, and a part of him wants to utter a string of profanity long enough to fill a spool, but he remains utterly still, his eyes locked on Shine.

She breaks away from his stare to watch his hands as she applies the gauze. Her lips are curled into a thoughtful frown.

"*Am* I dreaming?" she asks quietly. "None of this feels real."

"It is," he says softly. "And it will. Just give it time."

Chapter Six

It's almost midnight when Tatterdemalion wakes to the sound of screaming. In a heartbeat he's on his feet and throwing open the window to summon the wind. Seconds later he jumps down from Shine's windowsill.

She's still in bed, still gasping and howling, wrestling with her blanket as though it's trying to smother her. Her hands are clawed and she rakes her nails down her arms and shoulders, leaving thick welts in their path.

"Shine!" he says, catching her hands before she can hurt herself again. "*Shine!*" With a thought, the candle on the bedside bursts into flame, illuminating them both.

She stops thrashing, but every inch of her is shaking. Her eyes are wide and swollen, her face red with tears, and she stares at him in incomprehension

"Tatter?" Her voice is hoarse and small.

Gently he releases her hands. "I'm right here."

"I—I—" She stares at the blankets. "I thought they were—"

"Nothing but bedding here, Shine." He crouches low beside her. "You're in my care. I won't let anything happen to you."

"I know." She swallows several times before she manages to collect herself, and she attempts to slip back into the decorum of a duke's daughter. "I apologize for waking you."

"Think nothing of it," he says, matching her. "If you need me, just call."

He doesn't hear from her again that night, but not for lack of need. By morning, her eyes are red-rimmed and bloodshot, her feet drag, and even her patent stubbornness isn't enough to keep her head high.

"More bad dreams, Shine?" he asks, shepherding her away from the kitchen. She's in no state to touch a carving knife.

"Maybe one or two." She stifles a yawn. "No more than that."

They both know it's a lie.

For days she's weighed down by exhaustion, but she refuses to sit and rest, even after the sun has long gone down.

"I'm fine," she tells him, pressing on as only she can. "And I need to clean the library. Really, Tatter, you've let it fall apart while I've been away."

"That sounds like a chore for the morning, then," he says.

"Nonsense. I'm sure I could clean it in a few minutes. An hour, at most."

An hour, at most has a terrible habit of becoming two, then three, and then four, until the moon is high and she can barely make it up the steps to her bedroom.

"Not tonight," he says, and he hurries on before she has the chance to dig her heels in. "Do what you want to the library tomorrow, but tonight I need your assistance with a spell."

Her eyes narrow. "At this hour?" she asks, ignoring the fact that she had insisted on rearranging the bookshelves only a few minutes before.

"It's a nocturnal spell. Protection against unpleasant dreams."

She crosses her arms over her chest, her gaze dark. "I didn't realize my sleeping habits were such an inconvenience to you."

"Inspiration, really," he says lightly. "I hardly think you're the only one who has trouble sleeping, Shine. I imagine there are quite a few out there who might pay handsomely for a peaceful night's rest."

"Perhaps," she admits reluctantly.

"It will need some adjustment first, though," he says. "Would you care to help me test it?"

"You can come in now."

When Tatterdemalion steps through the door into her quarters, Shine is sitting in bed, her knees tucked to her chin, her fingers plucking absently at the hem of her nightgown. It's a soft, silvery gray fabric, woven from November mist and the sound of rain on windowpanes, and it carries with it all the comfortable drowse of a rainy day.

Shine doesn't look drowsy, though. There's apprehension in the curve of her back and the careful way she watches him.

He pulls up a chair close to her bed and takes a seat. "Nervous?"

"Of course not. I'm just wondering if it will work."

He presses a hand to his chest in feigned affront. "Have you lost faith in me already? I'm hurt."

"If you're that confident, then by all means," she says. "Let's see this spell of yours."

"Let me see your face," he says, leaning in. For a long moment she stares him down, and then she closes her eyes and tilts her face toward him.

His touch is light on her skin, his fingertips barely touching her forehead as he draws the runes. The staves are elaborate, and he traces magic into every line. As he draws, Shine's brow loses its tense furrows and her shoulders sag.

"Would you like to lay down?" Tatterdemalion murmurs.

She hums a wordless affirmative, and he pulls away to let her settle in properly. Her lids are heavy, and she pulls the down comforter close to her chin with a small yawn.

As soon as she's comfortable, he leans in and continues the spell, tracing intent over intent and line over line. One arm is propped against his knee, his wrist dangling uselessly near the bed. He doesn't even notice it there until Shine's hand closes around his.

The spell is wrapped around her like an embrace, easing her off to sleep. Only a few more lines, and he'll be finished.

But before he can trace the last few lines on her brow, she mumbles three words: "Stay with me."

It was barely whispered, maybe not even said aloud, but it burns through his skin and sinks into his bones. The magic of the ring won't let him refuse.

He squeezes her hand gently. "Don't worry, Shine. I'll be here."

Shine's command starts itching under his skin when he gets as far as the door. A few steps further, and it turns into sharp, stabbing pains that run down his limbs and constrict his lungs. A few steps beyond that, and he'll be gasping and writhing on the floor, but he doesn't test his limits that far.

His experiments are interrupted by a whimper from across the room. Shine is fidgeting in her bed, her face contorted like she's in pain.

He takes a seat at Shine's side and lays his hand over her forehead. The spell he crafted isn't flawed so much as it is incomplete: it keeps her asleep and guards against proper dreams, but memories are another matter. He traces new staves of peace and escape into her skin, urging the nightmarish memories to fade.

Slowly the tension drains from Shine's features, and she falls back into a gentle slumber. Relaxation softens her features, but her face never quite loses the hard lines and sharp angles that define her. The word he would use isn't *beautiful* so much as *striking*—and he suspects she would approve of the substitution. The thought makes him smile.

Unable to leave, he occupies his time observing the room he's currently trapped in. It's cramped and plain, just whitewash and plaster on top of wood and stone, with a small fireplace and a window barely large enough to step through. Drafts leak through the rafters and the splintering window frame, enough that he can smell the storm gathering around them before its dark clouds blot out the stars.

Thunder rolls around them: a long, low growl that vibrates the floor under his feet. Shine makes a small noise, not quite stirring from sleep.

"No, you don't," he tells the storm. "She's gone long enough without rest."

It replies with a sharp crack that rattles the window panes. Tatterdemalion doesn't give it a second warning.

Without properly thinking about it he throws open a window and reaches into the coming storm—and then he draws it inside, plucking it from a raindrop like a fiber of wool from a ball of roving. He wraps his magic tight around it, braiding in the sound of thunder, the smell of rain in the trees, the billowing clouds, until all that's left outside is the soft rhythm of rainfall around them.

He summons first the spinning wheel, then the loom, and then his needle and scissors, whiling away the hours with the familiar rhythm of his work.

Shine finally awakes hours after dawn, looking more rested than she has in days.

Tatterdemalion waits until she finishes stretching and yawning before he announces his presence. "Well. You're certainly looking better."

She jolts upright. "What are you doing here?"

You asked me to stay doesn't feel like a good enough answer. "Checking on the spell, of course. And making a delivery." He gestures to the table on the far corner, and tentatively she approaches it.

"What is this?" she whispers, running her hands over fabric as soft as the clouds it was woven from.

"It stormed last night," he says by way of answer. "I thought it suited you." He gestures to the door, silently asking permission to leave. "Shall I let you try it on?"

She nods quickly, and he can feel the previous command release him from its grip.

He would leave—he has sleep of his own to catch up on, after all—but he lingers outside the door until she pulls it open. The dress really does suit her: storm clouds billow in the folds of her skirt and drift across her bodice. Arcs of lightning cross the fabric when she moves, safe now though they're not yet tamed, and when they leave her dress they dance in her hair.

"Thank you." The words come out as barely a breath. "It's incredible."

"Does it fit well?" he asks lightly, but he already knows the answer.

The night he spent working feels like a fair price for the sight of her smile.

The castle is almost blinding by day.

The curtains are gone from the windows, hanging like flags in the courtyard to dry after a ruthless scrubbing. Since then, Shine has declared war against the dust and grime that's accumulated in the past year, beaten the rugs within an inch of existence, and polished every surface until it gleams.

"I could help—" Tatterdemalion begins.

"Let me do it," she snaps, perhaps too sharply. He doesn't ask again.

He never once asked her to do any of it, but she can't make herself stop. It feels like a compulsion, like if she scrubs hard enough she'll wash away the last year and come back to where she was before the tower. And if she can't do that, she'll settle for having this little ounce of control. She can't save herself from Bryony, but she can save this castle from a little bit of dirt.

It feels like a shallow victory, but she'll take what she can get.

Now she's mopping—at least, she's dragging the mop across the floor and gathering up grime that hasn't yet had time to accumulate.

Tatterdemalion approaches slowly, addressing her from a distance so he doesn't catch her by surprise.

"You're doing it differently," he remarks.

She glares, her mouth pursed in preparation for a challenge. "I just mopped there."

"Why, so you did." He gives a cursory glance at the footsteps he left on the still-wet floor. To his credit, his shoes are impeccably clean. "But that does not address the more *pressing* concern."

She raises an eyebrow, inviting him to continue.

"You used to do it much better."

"Really?" she asks. "And how's that?"

He twists his face into a mockery of outrage. "You used to dance when you mopped."

She blinks, her defense forgotten. "I did not."

"Oh yes, you did. And now there is a disgraceful lack of dancing in this house. I will not have it."

She recovers herself in an instant, and she's absolutely not taking his bait. "Why don't you throw a ball, then, if you're so starved for dance?"

He makes a face.

"No? Then allow me to introduce you to your new dance partner." She pushes the mop at him, curtsying to the handle. "Her Grace says her card is empty this evening."

He bows to the mop with a flourish. "A pleasure as always, Your Grace." Then he takes it from her and begins a lively reel, dragging the mop with him across the floor. Despite her sour mood, Shine can't quite hide her smile. Tatterdemalion doesn't even bother hiding his.

When he makes a second pass, the air fills with grand music to match the beat of his steps. He whirls away from the mop; it keeps flopping, though now it's joined by a gentlemanly coat rack. Tatterdemalion doesn't give Shine a chance to turn away before he sweeps her up into the dance.

"Time to switch partners," he says with a sly grin, and she's too busy laughing to refuse. She can't remember the last time she's danced with a proper partner, but her feet still remember the steps even though her head doesn't. Tatterdemalion guides her effortlessly, grinning so wide his eyes sparkle.

"I've never seen you dance before," she says.

"I'm sure you've never seen a clock dance, either," he returns. Half his furniture and most of his wardrobe has descended to the floor, joining them in an impromptu ball.

She moves tightly against him, her bodice sliding across his doublet as they dance. She feels like she's burning up, but his hands are soothing and cool. Her heartbeat races and he pulls her closer, moving faster, the music picking up speed to keep up with their own maddened paces.

The world has vanished around them, a cyclone of color and light. It feels like something out of a dream, too wonderfully absurd to be real, and she wants nothing more than to let it go on forever.

He's close enough that she can taste his breath, and she lets herself lean in closer.

Kiss me.

She didn't say it aloud—she knows she didn't—but he startles as if she blurted the words out in front of him. He stumbles, and in the half beat it takes him to recover, he's tripled the distance between them.

There's a strange look on his face, but she can't read it before he dips into a sweeping bow. He brings her hand to his lips, pressing a kiss to her knuckles and lingering there a few moments longer than necessary.

A flush heats her cheeks, but even she doesn't know why. A kiss on the hand is a greeting, a courtesy, a sign of respect—but in that moment it feels like flirtation and rejection and dismissal all at once. Lightning radiates down her dress, echoing her confusion.

Tatterdemalion sees every moment of it. He's watching her through his lashes.

"I should let you finish your work," he says, and the next moment he's gone.

Chapter Seven

Tatterdemalion paces his laboratory in maddening circles. He told himself he needs to check which supplies need to be restocked, but that's a lost cause. The list he made is entirely illegible: the letters crawl across the parchment in every direction like a nest of frightened vipers, unicorn blood has been repeated four times, and fire salamander skin appears twice, along with half a dozen other ingredients that have been repeated.

His mind keeps going back to that dance and all the things it shouldn't mean.

Shine wanted him to kiss her—wanted it so intensely that the ring took it as a command—and he *wanted* to do it, damn all the consequences.

But there *would* be consequences.

If he kisses her now, that would be the end. His contract with the demon would be broken. After hundreds of years of power and immortality, time would start for him again.

The ancient, demonic part of him rails against it. He has too many enemies, knows too many secrets, owns too many treasures. If he loses his power now, the whole world will descend on him, and he'll be defenseless to fight it off. If not men and monsters, then old age will eventually kill him.

And then what will become of you?

He pauses to glance out the window. Shine is in the courtyard, wrapped in a cloak of living fire and trying to persuade the wind to let her ride it. It's an impossible task, of course—the only reason Tatterdemalion can do it at all is because of the demon's power—but of all people, she might actually be able to do it. She's stubborn enough, and the wind seems to have taken a liking to her.

It's nipping at her cloak with an odd enthusiasm. It's practically shoving her across the courtyard toward the doors of the keep.

He frowns. Shine's strong, but there's no reason for it to be that rough with her, even in play.

The next gust almost knocks her off her feet. It isn't playing.

He pulls open the window, and a frantic gale drags at his hair and forces him to look toward the gate. There are people moving toward the castle. They're staying off the main road, hidden far enough behind the line of trees that they're barely visible if he isn't looking directly at them. He can't tell how many there are, but they're close. Far too close.

The great gate is shut, but unlocked. With a furrow of his brow, he issues the command to bar it against intruders.

The gate does nothing. There's an oddly familiar absence where its obedience should be.

It takes half a moment for him to recognize it.

"Shine!" he shouts, leaping onto the windowsill and summoning the wind to his side. "Shine, get inside!"

He doesn't know if she hears him. She whirls around to face the great gate, just in time to see it flung open.

From here, Tatterdemalion can see a series of symbols carved into the wood. He knows them well: the last time he saw them, they were burned into Shine's skin.

The memory has barely an instant to register before the courtyard is flooded with attackers. More than a dozen men pour in, wearing the mismatched garb of those who scavenge off their kills. In a heartbeat, they have Shine surrounded.

She's well within her rights to scream. Instead she stands tall, looking the nearest imperiously in the eyes.

"Who are you?" she demands. "How dare you approach this castle?" Every last one of them is armed—some with knives and some with clubs. One seems to be holding a butcher's meat hook.

"You hear that, boys?" laughs a man with a particularly ornate dagger in his hand. "The lady wants to know how dare we." A chorus of ill-mannered guffaws answer him, like the cackle of crows. He twists the dagger so she can see the runes etched into the blade. "Might have something to do with this right here, maybe. Might have something to do with a little secret we learned. Wanna guess what it is?"

Shine looks ill, but she doesn't cower. "That won't save you. Leave this place at once." Her command, meant for other ears, slides harmlessly past Tatterdemalion as he descends to the courtyard.

"Sure, we'll leave," says another man. "As soon as we get what we came for." He flashes a leering grin. "I hear there's treasure here. Enough to keep a man rich and fat for centuries."

"Look at that cloak," another one mutters, creeping up behind her. "You could buy a horse with a cloak like that. That's magic, it is."

He starts forward, but doesn't get close enough to grab her.

No, he would need *bones* for that. And at the moment, the man is no more than a puddle of skin and sinew. His club might be etched with those damned runes, but his flesh isn't.

Shine lunges for the remains of the bandit and seizes his knife. Two more charge at her, and she slashes wildly.

Screams fill the clearing, Shine's among them. But even as she screams she's fighting—kicking, clawing, thrashing and stabbing. Leaping into the fray, Tatterdemalion dances among her attackers, turning this one to stone, burning that one alive, trapping that one over there inside a tree that grows up around him in the blink of an eye.

And then he stops.

The ring's magic tightens around him, knotting his muscles and freezing his bones, tangling the threads of his power at the tips of his fingers. He's frozen, helpless to do anything but stare.

Shine is on the ground. One of the largest of the bandits stands over her, his shirt cut and torn from her attack, the magic ring in his hands.

The blood freezes in Tatterdemalion's veins as he looks into the eyes of his new master.

"So now you're scared, are ye?" the bandit growls. He inches toward Shine. Tatterdemalion can't move, but his eyes narrow. Rage scorches his senses. "Who's this, then? Your sweetheart? She important to you? Must be, if you gave her this little trinket." He twists the ring in front of him. "I've got a message for you from the one that sent us. There's a Magpie out there who don't like you keeping shiny things all to yourself."

The compulsion loosens around Tatterdemalion's mouth. He can speak again, but only to answer. He doesn't trust himself to form words. From the corner of his eye he glimpses Shine crawling to her knees, all but forgotten.

"How 'bout we make a deal, eh?" the bandit says. A nervous laughter creeps up around the his two remaining fellows as they eye their dead. "You stay nice and far away, and we won't do anything to this pretty little dear. How's—" His gloating curdles into a scream as Shine's dagger carves deep into his thigh. Before he can catch his breath, she yanks the blade out and buries it in his throat. He drops like a shot bird and Shine stands over him, her face white, her fingers still wrapped around the bloodstained knife.

She turns slowly, ever so slowly, to face the last two men. The knife is in her hands. Her hair is wild. Lightning and flame crackle in her clothes.

Her breath comes in gasps, but her voice is steady and deadly calm: "I suggest you leave."

Outmatched and alone, they don't need to be told a second time.

She stands tall, watching them flee until they pass the tree line. As soon as they're out of sight, her knees begin to shake and she sinks to the ground. Tatterdemalion materializes under her, catches her, and guides her to clear ground away from the bodies.

He won't ask her if she's all right. He knows better than that.

"Did they hurt you?" he asks instead, his voice too low in her ear.

"What—" She sounds faint, and he draws her tighter against him. "What are you going to do to them?"

He's already memorizing their faces in preparation for the curses that he'll send after them. "Whatever you want me to do, Shine."

She buries her face in his shoulder, and he can feel the tremors there, the spreading dampness as she tries and fails to keep herself from crying.

"Leave them. Let them go." Sobs thicken her voice, but there's strength in it.

Even without the ring's command, he can't make himself refuse.

He sets her down by the fire and returns to the courtyard. At his command, the earth rises up and pulls the bodies under the grass, leaving nothing behind but their enchanted weapons and a single golden ring.

He bends to pick it up, turning it over in his hand. After all this time, it's finally back in his control. He lets it linger in his palm for a moment before he returns inside and presses it into Shine's hand without a word.

She looks up at him. The tears have dried and the shock has faded, and she wears the recent fear on her shoulders like a lion's pelt.

"I want to know exactly what that was."

"Those were bandits," he says. "Nothing more."

"They were working for the Sorcerer Queen." Her lips are drawn into a thin line. "I saw those symbols they were using—they were hers. I want to know why they came here."

There are a hundred thousand answers to that question, but only one that matters: "She wanted to send a message."

"I heard," she says. "Something about a magpie?"

He shakes his head. "That wasn't the message, it was just the signature." The real message is carved into his great gate. "She wanted me to know that she can come in here any time she wants. This castle isn't safe from her anymore."

They pack lightly, only the clothes on their back and a few trinkets that are too dangerous to leave behind. Tatterdemalion stows most of them in his bottomless pockets, but Shine takes the basilisk venom from the shelf and tucks it into her belt. What they can't carry is locked into the treasure rooms before they're sealed with layers of magic and solid stone.

Within an hour, Tatterdemalion summons the wind to carry them away. Soon the castle is gone, vanished in the distance. A mountain swells below them, and the wind weaves them between the climbing peaks of an entire range until it too falls away out of sight. The land flattens, leveling until it sinks into the sea, and finally even the shoreline vanishes over the horizon. The sea is vast and flat in all directions, interrupted only by a single ship.

It seems tiny, alone on the water, but as they draw closer, the *Devil's Bargain* seems to swell before them, with sails large enough to enshroud houses, hung from masts that might just be entire trees. Every visible surface is alive with men and women who rush around each other in eclectic disarray. None of them react to Tatterdemalion or Shine, even when the wind deposits them on the deck.

Shine frowns at them, too dizzy to put the question to words. After hours hurtling through the air, the lurching rhythms of a ship at sea leave her disoriented. Tatterdemalion struggles with the same, and he's had hundreds of years to get accustomed to the feeling.

"Invisibility," Tatterdemalion explains, steadying her with a hand on the small of her back.

"I assumed that much." She braces herself against him. "But why are we here?"

He flashes a grim grin. "There's safety in the sea, Shine. If Bryony wants to bring her armies here, she'll have to load them onto boats first, and that will take time. More than enough time for us to make ourselves scarce somewhere else. Besides, the good captain owes me a favor. And there he is now!" He pulls away and steps immediately behind the captain, revealing himself at precisely the right moment for dramatic effect. Even before he unveils Shine, he can feel her stare burning into him.

It doesn't take long to persuade Captain Danova to take them on as passengers—after all, Tatterdemalion raised his ship from the bottom of the sea, and he has no compunctions against sending it back. As a show of faith, the captain even settles them in his own quarters while the sailors empty a private cabin for their use.

"Shall I prepare a second cabin for your..." He hesitates for half a moment, glancing at Shine. "Guest?"

Before Tatterdemalion can answer, Shine does it for him. "That won't be necessary."

With a look, he signals for the captain to do as she says. He doesn't question it until Danova is gone and the door sealed behind him.

"This is quite a large ship," he muses. "There's no need to risk your reputation when you could have a room to yourself."

"Your apprentice sent bandits to murder me this morning, and you think I'm concerned for my image?" She seats herself on the bed, her cloak spread behind her like a curtain of flame. "Let these sailors think I'm your lover. It might persuade them to keep their hands to themselves."

"Not to worry about that," he says. "I'll make sure to—"

"I'm more concerned about Bryony." Her expression is unyielding. "She was your apprentice, wasn't she? Why would she attack the castle?"

"That isn't important at the moment," he says.

"You've said that already." Her posture shifts just slightly, and his heart sinks. He's all too familiar with the look of her digging her heels in. "You said there were more pressing matters to deal with. You said our first priority was escape." She raises her hand, indicating the captain's quarters. "By the look of it, we've escaped. So answer the question."

"You're insufferable," he mutters.

"I'm aware." She fixes him with a stare as unrelenting as the sea itself. "She came after me. I have a right to know why."

It's a question Tatterdemalion has been trying not to answer for far too long, and an answer that has been growing all the more solid the longer he's avoided thinking of it.

He heaves a grudging sigh. "The reasons are... *complicated.*"

"It seems we suddenly have a great deal of time on our hands." She narrows her eyes. "Elaborate, if you please."

He's met mountains with less resolve, and so he allows himself to cave in. "There's something I have that she wants. I believe she thinks she can use you to take it from me."

Shine scowls. "After everything she did to me, you still think I'm a spy?"

"Not so directly. Not knowingly. It wouldn't work if you knew."

"Well, then that seems like an excellent way to thwart her plans, doesn't it? What exactly is it that she doesn't want me to know?"

Tatterdemalion shrinks into himself. She's right, and he knows it, but the thought of telling her leaves a pit in his stomach.

It won't work if she knows. That was what saved him from his Magpie, once upon a time.

"When she was my apprentice, she realized that there was a limit to what I could teach her. No matter how she tried, certain powers would forever be beyond her grasp. She knew that kind of magic had to be possible, because I could do it, but she could never quite manage what I had done."

He can see it in Shine's eyes: she knows precisely what he's talking about. She might be able to coax fire and water to do her bidding, but he can pull thunderstorms and birdsongs from the air.

"It consumed her. She delved into darker and darker places, searching for the key. I thought by telling her the truth I could save her."

"The truth," Shine says carefully.

"That the things I can do don't come because of some secret spells that I've been keeping from her. It wasn't the study of magic that made me this way, Shine." He pulls each word out like a rotten tooth and sets it before her to see. "I am the host of a demon."

If she were anyone else, he might expect her to flinch or back away. Not Shine. Her stare is unwavering.

"It was dying," he says. "I was able to force it into a deal, to give me its power without stealing my autonomy. It was an arrangement of chance and desperation, and she'll never be able to repeat it, no matter how often she's tried. She will never be more powerful than I am now."

"She doesn't have to be," Shine mutters. "She conquered half a continent with the power she already has. You didn't stop her."

No, he didn't—because stopping her would mean looking her in the eyes again. It would mean begging on his knees, pleading for her to put this behind her. And if that didn't work, it would mean putting an end to her reign permanently.

He can't do it.

He can't kill her.

And he knows that's entirely according to her plan.

"It's a tenuous position," he says carefully. "Just because I didn't doesn't mean I won't. So she intends to make sure that I can't." He hesitates. "There is an... artifact. One that she could use to control me. I think she wanted you to steal it from me—and then once you had it, I imagine she intended to kill you and take it off your corpse."

He can stop it here. He doesn't need to tell her another word. His answer should more than satisfy her.

He continues anyway.

"But it's not the only way. When I made my bargain with the demon, I insisted on an escape clause to our contract. Something I had assumed would be easy, and the demon assumed would be all but impossible. If I fulfil it, the demon will be gone forever." He hesitates around the words. "And my powers with it."

"What was it?" she asks, barely audible.

The question hangs between them for too long. He's told her too much already for him to back out now, but he still wants to put it off as long as possible, as if waiting just a little longer might change it.

But it won't. All the time in the world won't change it.

"A kiss," he says at last. "From someone who loves me."

It seemed like such an odd stipulation when he made the deal. An unnecessary bit of detail thrown in because demons have a taste for the specific.

It took him centuries to realize it was a trick.

He fell in love with his Magpie. Hopelessly, desperately, blindingly in love. When she asked him to spend the rest of his life with her, he accepted without hesitation, powers be damned. He kissed her, fully prepared to look at her through mortal eyes.

But when he pulled away, nothing had changed. Magic still coursed in his veins. The demon still thrummed in the back of his head.

And his Magpie was not hurt, not disappointed, but *outraged* that it didn't work. It couldn't work—not with her. Because she didn't love him.

So she left, and she conquered nations, and she waited with all the patience of a carrion bird circling over a dying beast.

"Her greatest strength is her understanding of potential, you see. She doesn't lay foundations, so much as she plants seeds in fertile soil, cultivates them when they show promise, and harvests them when they come to fruition." He's vain enough to believe that he taught her that technique, but she's the one who perfected it. "You were known for buying books on magic, once. Merchants came from lands unnumbered to sell to you. Did you really think you escaped her notice?"

Shine clenches her teeth.

"Did you think it was random happenstance that of all the creatures that might have taught you magic, your book taught you to summon me?"

"You think she sent me the book."

"I think she intended for me to be your teacher."

"Why?" Shine demands, incredulous. "So I could fall in love with you?" The words drip off her tongue like venom, acrid with disdain, and he recalls the feeling of basilisk fangs sinking into his chest.

He's not certain when he started to hope. He doesn't allow emotion to show on his face as the feeling dissolves into nothing.

"When you didn't," he continues as if nothing has changed, "she tried to crush the magic out of you before you could become another rival." He tilts his head, sardonic. "She knows me well enough to predict me. I think she has no idea how to handle you."

It's not the only thing that makes her a threat.

Shine killed one of Bryony's men and summoned Tatterdemalion to help her escape. For Shine's sake, he killed dozens of Bryony's soldiers and the bandits she sent to do her bidding.

For the first time since his Magpie left him, he's acted against her.

For the first time since he laid eyes on her, he's no longer under her control.

The realization comes abruptly. It doesn't matter that Shine doesn't love him. He doesn't care. He'll still do what he can to protect her, ring or no.

His gaze flits down to her hand, and his thoughts freeze in his skull.

Her hand is bare.

"Shine," he asks quietly. "The ring I gave you. Where is it?"

She looks at her finger, quizzical. "I... I don't know."

"You had it here, didn't you?" he asks.

He remembers picking it up off the ground. Handing it to her. But she was in shock at the time—did she even put it on?—and then they were running, because it was only a matter of time before Bryony arrived.

"I don't—" All at once, understanding dawns on her features. "The artifact you were talking about."

He doesn't answer. Judging by the look on her face, he doesn't have to.

"Why would you give something like that to me?" she asks.

Another question he'd rather not answer. As it turns out, he doesn't have the chance. Because before he can open his mouth, he feels a command carving through him with white-hot intensity.

Come here.

For a moment he's blind and reeling, aware only of the sudden cold and the stone under his knees. When his vision clears he sees the familiar lines of his castle, the room that had once been his.

The Sorcerer Queen considers him carefully, a smile on her too-red lips as she twirls his ring in her hands.

Chapter Eight

Weeks become months.

Bryony has planted her own throne in Tatterdemalion's grand hall, taken the room that used to be his, and sequestered him to his old laboratory. It isn't as though he can't make the place more comfortable—she doesn't care nearly enough about his daily affairs to keep him from sealing drafts and smoothing stone—but she's already stolen the only comforts he might have had.

The embroidered shirt is nothing but ashes now, thrown into the fire by his own hands at her command. The dresses Shine wore are torn to shreds, their magic reworked into more practical spells.

His only solace is that Shine is gone, too far away for Bryony to bother with, so long as he behaves. And so he behaves. He puts down uprisings. Sinks entire cities into the sea. Murders dissenters by the dozens and arranges their heads on pikes like flowers in a bouquet. The tasks might not have bothered him once, but every new act leaves him repulsed.

He can't refuse. He can't escape. He can't even resist anymore.

When he starts to rebel, when magic crackles at his fingertips, ready to crush and tear and burn, she pouts at him with a sweet, heartless smile.

"It's getting absolutely filthy in here, Tatter. Do you think we should bring back that girl of yours?"

Her words bind him better than shackles or magic ever could.

The wind plucks at his hand and tugs at his hair, rustling with secret news. It knows where Shine is hidden, but he won't let it tell him.

Bryony can tell when he does, and her lips curve into a calculated smile.

"Tell me," she says. "How is dear Shine?" And the command squeezes the truth out of his throat.

Better to say "I don't know". Better to leave her without ammunition. Better to wither alone in the dark than to drag Shine down with him.

There's no command Shine can give to make Captain Danova turn his ship around. The trade winds are in their favor, the hull is heavy with dichroic glass and Tussar silk, and they'll need to stop soon to resupply. He isn't willing to risk a profitable venture on a passenger's whim, especially not when she demands he take her into waters controlled by the Sorcerer Queen.

"I'm sorry, *ricahembra*," he tells her. "If the Magister wants to go back there, that's his business. But if that woman's made you her enemy, then returning is certain death. And I'd rather not see what your friend will do to me and my crew if I help you get yourself killed."

She stares him in the face. If he won't take her, she'll find another way.

"Very well," she said. "But if I must wait for him here, then at least give me something to do."

He's taken aback by the request. "I'm afraid we don't have much to do on this ship befitting a lady."

"That's fine." And she turns an expression on him that he knows he can't fight. "Show me the makings of a sailor, and I'll show you what *I* make of it."

Warily he has his men teach her to mend nets. Her fingers fumble and blister over the work, but she throws herself into it until she knows the motions as easily as breathing and can twist wanting and impatience into each of the knots. The sailors soon learn to tell which nets are hers: they're always the ones that have to be pulled from the sea quickly, before they're full to the point of breaking. When she sets foot on the upper deck, the wind strains against the sails, pushing the ship faster and farther than it should rightfully go. One of the cabin boys even swears that he saw lower decks mop themselves when she was tasked with cleaning them. When they make port in the city of Umarah, more than a few of the sailors try to persuade her to stay on with them—she's good luck, they say.

She takes her leave all the same.

The market in Umarah is vast and thriving. While Captain Danova loads his hull with wine and argan oil and saffron threads, she ventures into the deepest alleys and backstreets, where merchants sell sea serpent scales and leviathan eyes. Her fire cloak is traded for a dagger, a spot on a caravan, and gold that she stitches into the linings of her clothes. For a month she travels with merchants on camelback; she learns to fight from a guard with piercing eyes, and learns medicine from an old midwife who has crossed the sand a thousand times before.

When the caravan takes her as far north as it will go, she trades her thunderstorm gown for a horse and saddle and a month's supplies, and she rides. The days grow shorter as desert dunes stretch into vast plains, and they in turn rise into mountains. She's deep into the Duenna mountain range when the first winter storm hits, leaving her stranded in a little town at the edge of a mountain pass. She sells the horse to a blacksmith in return for a place to stay and a season's apprenticeship. The things she makes lack her master's elegance and craft, but they have a particular resilience—a stubbornness beaten into every inch of iron.

Her work is good, and when the spring comes, the blacksmith warns her not to take the treacherous mountain paths, still prone to floods from the melting snow. Instead he brings her to the miners who sell him his iron. In exchange for weeks with a pickaxe, the miners promise to show her the tunnels that will take months off her journey. It's not long before they notice the way fire obeys her command, and so they teach her to use the blasting powder that breaks up the stone. When they lead her from the mountains, she takes a bundle of it with her, along with their blessing.

On the other side of the mountains, the countryside is more familiar, and she marches on with more confidence.

One vision haunts her: the look on Tatterdemalion's face before he disappeared, the shock and hurt and, if she didn't know better, fear.

The thought chills her. Because anything that could frighten Tatterdemalion...

She doesn't like to think about it. Instead she focuses her energy on walking, mile after mile, moor after mountain, crossing the vast expanse one step at a time. With little of value left to her name, she lives by begging at night, she sleeps under trees, she drinks from streams. Sometimes painful thoughts cross her mind—that he came back to the ship where he left her, that she wasn't there, that he'll think she abandoned and betrayed him when all she wants is to find him again.

She tries not to think of that either.

Chapter Nine

Months have passed since he's seen her. Longer than that, though Tatterdemalion doesn't let himself keep track. Bryony says she's made his castle into her summer home, and they've only come back here twice. A year then, maybe two.

The wind plucks listlessly at his hair through the open window, like a disembodied hand petting a beaten dog. But suddenly that hand seizes him.

He cringes, bracing against the pull of the ring, but no command follows. It's just the wind.

A moment later, the protective wards around the castle crackle and flare. He strides to the windowsill and sees a lone figure approaching on the main road. She's dressed in rags, a hood low over her face, a traveling pack heavy on her shoulders. She might be a beggar, but there is no humility in the way she carries herself.

He knows her in an instant.

His first impulse is to run to her, to gather her up in his arms and hold her until the sun goes cold.

But that impulse dies quickly, buried beneath panic and horror. She needs to leave. She needs to get away. She was safe on the sea, far away in the distant lands. Why couldn't she have stayed there?

But it's too late. The doors are already opening, and Bryony's guards are already coming out to meet her.

"Identify yourself," says the captain of the guard.

Shine intended to pass herself off as a flower seller, but that plan dies the moment she passes the wards. She can feel them burn against her skin like the memories of red-hot iron.

Bryony's men surround her, their weapons drawn like she's an intruder. The castle knows better. The well burbles in recognition, and she calls the water up through the earth to meet her, soaking the ground around her feet.

She stands tall. "I'm here to see the Sorcerer Queen."

"I said identify yourself," the captain of the guard says, louder this time. A sword is leveled at her face.

Shine shuts her eyes and lets out a held breath. She knows the give of steel under a blacksmith's hammer, the weight of raw ore piled high in a mining cart, and she commands the sword to yield.

"Oh, there's no need for that." The doors of the keep swing open under their own power, and the master of the castle descends the steps to the courtyard. It's been more than a year since she was staring at Shine from the other end of a firebrand. In all that time, Bryony hasn't aged a day. "I remember her just fine. The girl who escaped the tower. What brings you to my castle, my dear?"

The wind rustles in her hair, urging her to look up. There, in the laboratory window: she spots him for half a moment before she turns her face back to the Sorcerer Queen.

"I've come to bargain." She pulls the pack off her shoulders. Tucked beneath a weathered sleeping roll is a miner's pickaxe.

"Your Majesty, the woman's armed!" The sword pointed at her is swung. In the tower window, Tatterdemalion leaps to his feet in alarm.

The blade strikes her back—then crumbles into rust and brittle slate. The guards try to rush at her, but their boots are swallowed past their ankles in deep mud. While they struggle to free themselves, Shine marches forward. From her pack she draws an iron ball the size of her fist.

"I've come to make a bargain," she repeats, louder this time.

"Let me see if I can guess," Bryony says. "You'll give me that ball if you I give you... a golden ring, perhaps?"

"I think you misunderstand me, Your Majesty," she says. "If you give me the ring, I'll let you leave this place alive."

"Consider my counter offer." With a sweep of her hand, Bryony summons the flames out of the fireplace into a roaring pillar and arches it over her head, sending it straight for Shine.

Shine hurls the iron ball into the fire and leaps to the side, taking shelter behind the stone wall half a breath before the blasting powder inside explodes.

The explosion cracks stone and leaves three men dead in its wake. The Sorcerer Queen only smirks, unscorched. "Fireworks, dear? You really should know better than to wear your weapons."

It's all the warning she gets before another arc of fire rounds the wall.

Shine rips off her travelling pack and throws it into the oncoming flame. Time seems to freeze as the Queen wraps a protective spell around herself. Shine pulls the earth itself over her head for shelter. The guards hit the floor. The pack explodes, bits of shrapnel embedding themselves in the far walls.

High in the tower, a command etches itself into Tatterdemalion's bones: **Come here**.

He's ready this time, and that means he can defy her, if only a little. He sets his face into a rictus and begins to walk, dragging his feet each step of the way. He'll delay as long as he can stand the pain. As long as he has to.

Below, the Sorcerer Queen frowns at his defiance, and then her lips curl into a wicked smile, as if she's thought of a joke.

"My, you really *are* serious, aren't you?" She shrugs. "Very well. Go see him, if he's so important to you."

Shine rises, wary, from her hiding place. She's got one last weapon clutched in her hand. Bryony merely sighs.

"No need for dramatics, child. He's in the tower. Nobody's going to stop you."

Shine's eyes go wide, and she sidles down the familiar paths, not trusting Bryony with her back.

When the Bryony's out of sight, she breaks into a run, taking the stairs two at a time.

Stay where you are, Tatterdemalion.

He isn't sure if it's the command that roots him in place, or the sight of the woman before him.

There she is, real and alive and whole and beautiful. The sun has darkened her face and added streaks of silver to her hair, now plaited to keep it out of her eyes; her hands have grown callused, and new muscle winds its way down her limbs.

He can't stop himself.

"Shine?" it comes out a croak. She breaks into a smile like sun after a storm, and rushes at him. It's all he can do to throw out his hands. "Shine, stop. You have to leave. You have to—"

"No, Tatterdemalion." She keeps walking, and his outstretched arms crumple against her waist. "I'm getting you out of here."

"Shine, please. You don't understand—"

"No, I don't. But I understand the only thing that matters." Her hands wrap around his neck. "Tatter—"

He sees her lips form the words, but he can't hear them. He can't hear anything but the cold laugh echoing inside his head.

Now kill her.

Chapter Ten

The Queen's command echoes in Tatterdemalion's skull, but she says it again anyway, for spite.

Kill her.

It digs into his skin like a fresh tattoo, twisting around his bones and burning into every fiber of muscle. His fingers twitch for her throat of their own accord; his hands shake even as he forces them to stay still.

Magic gathers at his fingertips, but he crosses the threads of devastation with memories of dance and laughter, leaving its power snarled and hopelessly tangled.

Shine stares up at him in alarm. He couldn't keep this off his face if he tried—every second of resistance is a firebrand in his core.

"Tatterdemalion?" Her voice is high and frightened. "What is it? What's wrong?"

How silly, he thinks, the thought numb despite the pain. *You should be worried for yourself.*

The shaking spreads, grows like a cancer. His knees buckle beneath him and he falls—would fall, except Shine's arms wrap around him, lower him to the floor as gently as she can. Comforting the man who's going to murder her. The irony of it hurts almost as much as the compulsion.

"Shine—" He can barely get out her name. His tongue rebels, trying to twist the syllable into the beginnings of a curse. "You need—to go. Run. Please. She—she'll make me kill you."

As though running away will save her. As though the compulsion will get any weaker if she's in faraway jungles or the bottom of the sea. He'll track her down, hunt her like an animal. Slaughter her.

And there's nothing either of them can do about it.

"I can't stop—*please, Shine*—"

But Shine pulls him closer, cradles him in her arms despite the convulsions. She's smiling, but her eyes glitter with tears as she takes his hand in her own. Pulls it to her chest. Lays it over her heart.

"It's alright," she whispers gently.

His traitorous fingers twitch. All he has to do is pull a single thread of magic. Stop her heart. It would be quick. Painless.

And then she'd be gone forever.

There has to be something he can trade, some deal he can strike. He'll level continents. He'll build galaxies. He'll beg. He'll die. Anything. Anything but this.

He pulls Shine down to him—he can't lift himself up to meet her anymore—and covers her lips with his own. His mouth is begging, pleading, even though he's shaking too hard to really feel her against him.

A scream fills his ears, and he presses harder against Shine. It's been centuries since he stopped caring about gods, but now he prays to every last one of them: *Don't take her away from me.*

Something shatters inside him like metal struck on stone. Vaguely he's aware of the throbbing pain of a heart as it beats for the first time in centuries. But he isn't paying attention to any of that.

Because he tastes blood in his mouth.

He doesn't want to look. Doesn't want to see if the kiss came too late. If he really killed her. The coward in him is looking for corners to hide in, shouting desperately for his demon and knowing it will never come back.

Another part of him can't stand not knowing. That part swallows the fear along with the taste of blood and the lump in his throat.

He opens his eyes.

Shine stares back at him. Her eyes are wide, her breaths heavy, her lips bruised from the intensity of the kiss. A trickle of blood flows from a fresh split where her lips were forced against her teeth, and he can't even think to be annoyed with himself.

She's alive.

Alive.

He shudders, suddenly cold and numb from relief, and lets his head fall to her shoulder. She holds him close, runs her hand over his back as though he's a child with a fever.

"Are you all right?" His voice is lower, huskier, than it's been in centuries. "Did I hurt you?"

"I'm fine," she whispers into his hair, and he can hear the smile in her voice. "What about you? Are you—"

Tatterdemalion feels the crackle of magic before he hears the familiar footsteps on the stone floor. Shine goes rigid, grabbing him tight against her chest. He has to crane his neck to see Bryony approach, her mouth curled into an annoyed smirk.

"Well. That's one way to do it." Bryony shrugs, her smirk turning feline and cruel. "I suppose congratulations are in order for the happy couple?"

"I appreciate the sentiment, Your Majesty," Shine says with a forced smile. She rises to her feet, pulling Tatterdemalion behind her. "Is there any chance of you letting us go, then?"

The Queen's lip curls. "Hardly."

"I'm sorry to hear that." Shine's shoulder hits the windowsill. She reaches into her pocket, and pulls out a glass vial.

Tatterdemalion knows that vial.

She hurls it into the Sorcerer Queen's face just as magic curls around Bryony's hand.

Tatterdemalion can see it there, feel the magic that's gathering around them. He sees the threads weave into a wall around the Queen, while others, like puppeteer's strings, wrap around Shine's throat.

There was a time when he would have been frozen in horror and indecision. But now Shine is before him, and he won't let anyone hurt her. Never again.

Bryony's defense is excellent, but now he can see the holes in it, the weaknesses. He doesn't have a demon's magic anymore, but he still has hundreds of years of experience to show him the little bits here and there that he need only *push*.

The shield protecting Bryony falls away.

The glass shatters under the weight of Shine's will, but for the instant that it's intact, Tatterdemalion recognizes the shape of the flask:

Basilisk venom.

Venom explodes through the air, flying in all directions. Tatterdemalion tries to pull Shine behind him, but he's knocked back by a sudden gale. The wind floods the chamber, driving the venom away from them and into Bryony.

For seconds, all they can hear is screaming.

Chapter Eleven

Once upon a time, a demon in need of a body found a woman dying in a tower.

"I can save you," it whispered into her ear. "Serve me, and you will have power beyond your imagination. Serve me, and you will have riches untold. Serve me, and you will never die."

She accepted its offer without a bargain. After all, it was all she had ever wanted.

"I think not." Shine bends down, careful to avoid the venom as she tugs the ring from Bryony's finger.

The Sorcerer Queen's eyes snap open in a face half-dissolved. She looses an unholy shriek and lunges for Shine—and then collapses back to the floor as if shackled.

"I said no." Mountains have bowed under that will. Here and now, Bryony is no different.

"You beast!" the Sorcerer Queen shrieks. "You monster! You—"

"Enough of that, too," Shine says, and Bryony's mouth clamps shut. She seethes wordlessly, her breath coming in hisses between clenched teeth and perforated cheeks.

Shine stares down at her, imperious as a queen. This is the woman who had her tortured and branded, who murdered her brother, who twisted half the world into chaos. She's had time to plan a thousand acts of revenge, and now Bryony is entirely within her power.

She swallows her bile and wraps her will around a command. "In the place where the Straits of Aintzane meet the Cosgun Sea there is an island that the sailors call Middleground. You are going to go there. You won't speak a word to anyone until you reach its shores. And you will stay there until I call on you again." She takes a step back, opening the way to the door. "Now go."

Shuddering, Bryony climbs to her feet and staggers out the door.

Tatterdemalion moves to the window, watching her as she crosses the courtyard and leaves the gate.

"Middleground?" he asks.

"I spent a few days there while the *Devil's Bargain* broke its mizzenmast in a storm," she says flatly. "I didn't particularly like it."

His brow is furrowed. It's strange seeing the emotion play so openly on his face. It's strange seeing him look human at all. "How long do you plan to keep her there?"

"Until I figure out something better to do with her." Outside, the deposed Sorcerer Queen passes out of sight. "Do you have anything in mind?"

Because Shine isn't the only one with a claim on Bryony. Her own feelings are singularly loathing, but she knows his will be infinitely more complicated.

"Whatever it is," he says, "I suggest we make a decision soon. That ring doesn't like being in one person's possession for long."

"So I've gathered." Already it's growing heavy in Shine's hand. It wants to escape—and if it does, there's no telling what havoc it will wreak. "Remind me, Tatter—isn't there a blacksmith's forge in the valley?"

The golden ring cannot be melted or beaten down, and so the two of them pour it into an iron ingot and bury it deep beneath the wine cellar in the castle, where it might never be found. They stay in the towers above, resting and recovering and clearing away the last of the wreckage of what was, until one day a messenger arrives at the castle door.

There are bandits on the roads, he tells them, and monsters in the woods. And above it all, the great bloated hulk of the Sorcerer Queen's empire is crumbling apart.

And Shine takes her Tatter's hand and says, "Let's see what we can do."

In the end, they don't live forever.

In the end, they don't have to.

About the Author

JW Troemner was born in Germany and immigrated to the United States, where she lives with her partner in a house full of pets. Most days she can be found gazing longingly at sinkholes and abandoned buildings.

www.ingramcontent.com/pod-product-compliance
Lightning Source LLC
Chambersburg PA
CBHW032012180726
48283CB00008B/2635